40 DAYS

MORGAN DEVIVO
40
DAYS

DEDICATION

To Chloe – The inspiration behind Elliana… our friendship has been tested too many times to count, yet we still manage to stick together through it all.

TABLE OF CONTENTS

ACKNOWLEDGEMENTS

I would like to thank the following for all that they've done and will continue to do along my journey…

To Mom and Dad and all of my amazing relatives up in New York. To my supportive group of friends who give me inspiration whether they realize it or not. To all of my teachers throughout the years who have fed my brain, fueled my passions, and put up with my bullshit (Auntie Tanya). To the whole team at 4 Horsemen Publications—thank you for taking a chance on me.

CHAPTER 1

There I was at the Haven Crest Mall. I honestly don't know how my sister, Mia Winterfield, managed to drag me into her shenanigans once again. Bribery is something I'll never understand. It's always, "If you take me to go clothes shopping, I'll buy you an ice cream at the food court." She never stays true to her word, yet I eat it up every time. Being seventeen and legally allowed to drive, living with a fourteen-year-old middle school sister is the worst. I'm basically a chauffeur who doesn't get paid, driving her friends around to parks and stores. Mia is a needy person, and she'll do anything to get what she wants, including using me until I'm worn down to a shell of the person I once was.

I stepped out of my black Nissan, exposed to the heat of the northwestern summer, and followed closely behind my sister. She was glammed up, like always, wearing a hot pink top and jeans. Designer sunglasses rested atop her head, nicely framing the side of her face. I must admit, I was a bit jealous.

"So, where are we off to first?" I asked.

"I need to get some perfume for back to school and a few new tops, maybe some nice jewelry, bath bombs, and a bit of décor for my room."

"Slow down—one thing at a time. Also, I don't think Mom's going to be very happy when you come home with a cart-full of t-shirts and other useless junk."

"Chill out, Stella. I have self-control," she snapped.

"Yep, sure ya do," I said, popping the "p."

As we walked toward the entrance of the mall, we passed by the nostalgic *Haven Crest* podium. It brought back a wave of memories from my childhood when Mia and I would go shopping with our grandma, taking pictures on Santa's lap during the winter and eating junky burgers at the food court. I missed the times when our relationship was simpler. We've been through some rough patches together, but the mall was always the place where we could forget about those problems, laughing as if we were little kids again.

As we stepped inside, the shopping center was a beautiful utopia of intricate architecture and trendy stores. Large glass ceilings stretched across the top of the structure, allowing natural sunlight to shine throughout. Meanwhile, rows of small shops displaying mannequins and decorative jewelry, trinkets and tiny treats flashed amidst the wave of customers. It was a large-scale building consisting of faceted gemstones which twinkled and gleamed shades of gold while chiseled travertine tiles accentuated the classy atmosphere. Elaborate arches curved the building into a similar form to that of a geodesic dome as its large plaza made way for a pleasurable and spacious environment. The smell of deep-fried donuts and burgers on the grill immediately took over my senses, making my stomach growl with a growing hunger. However,

Mia was insistent that we "follow the plan" and buy what she was there for.

I followed her around the first floor for a bit until we stopped at a quaint perfume shop. The outside was covered in an abundance of carnations and light chrysanthemums, and it smelled of sea salt, like a fresh ocean breeze. On the inside, pastel pink walls complimented the bottles of perfumes stacked upon the shelves, all illuminated by a twisty string of fairy lights. The store was nothing short of cozy. I let my sister wander around at her own discretion while I decided to peruse through the myriad of scents myself, captivated by the energy in the room. Botanical Garden, Salt Box, Wax Flower, Strawberry Fields—all unique perfumes which smelled comforting and left me with a fuzzy feeling in my chest. Suddenly, as I scanned the rows of spray-ons and body glitter, I was interrupted by a light tap on my shoulder.

"Done shopping already?" I asked, expecting to see my sister. Instead, when I turned around, I saw an unfamiliar girl around my age with short brown hair, wearing a sage-green collared blouse and brown button-up jeans. *Definitely not Mia.* I gave her a knowing laugh and shook my head in embarrassment. "Sorry, I thought you were someone else."

"That's fine. I actually wanted to ask you if you had any perfume recommendations? It's my first-time shopping here, and I don't know which one to buy," she said.

I furrowed my eyebrows and let out a confused chuckle. "I'm just as lost as you are. It's my first time here as well, but if I had to give you my unprofessional opinion, I'd say Wax Flower is pretty good."

She smiled at my response. "Thanks!"

"Yeah, no problem, but don't rely on me. That one over there in the pink is my sister Mia. She kind of dragged me in here."

"Sorry, I can't relate, being an only child and all. I'm sure your recommendation is better than anything I'd come up with on my own."

We both continued like this, making small talk for a while and forgetting about the world around us.

"By the way, my name's Elliana. Elliana Jones. I have been trying to make some new friends around the area, so maybe we can exchange numbers if you want and come to the mall another time," she said, reaching for her phone.

"For sure, that sounds great!" I responded, taking her phone and typing my number into the keypad. "I'm Stella, by the way."

Suddenly, Mia appeared and said she was ready to check out. I waved goodbye to Elliana, my sister eyeing me with a "Who is that?" face. I simply shrugged and said I would tell her when we got home.

Home. The word sounded so foreign to me. I didn't even know what it meant anymore. My dad died a few months ago, and on top of that, my mom got fired from her job, leaving me to be the only source of income for the family until she was able to get back on her feet. I worked 20 hours a week at a local retail store while still managing A+ grades in school. I was stressed out. I wanted to be anywhere else because home for me was just another stressful place. Thankfully, Mom got a new job, which meant that we didn't have to completely cut our spending anymore, hence why Mia saved up to go to the mall. But things still weren't good. My mom was awake at ungodly hours of the night, living off wine and other liquor. We were still stressed all the time. And now, with me about to start my senior year in high school, the pressure had only gotten worse. *I wish I could be anywhere but home.*

"So, Little Miss Popular is making friends everywhere she goes, huh?" My sister smirked as we continued to wander the floors of the mall.

"Oh shush, don't act like you haven't done the same," I joked, but in reality, my voice was tinged with a hint of seriousness. Mia attracted people everywhere she went with her trendy clothing style and bubbly mannerisms. Many of her friendships came from random encounters, a product of her charm and outgoing personality. I couldn't exactly relate. My introverted manner made me come off as rude and uninterested in the people around me, a stark contrast to my boisterous sibling. She was even pretty well known by the people in my own high school while I was occasionally referred to as "Mia's sister." *Such is the life of Stella Winterfield.*

After we were done at the perfume shop, Mia suggested we go looking for clothes. Or rather, *she* go looking for clothes. Her favorite store was located on the second floor of the building. As we rode the escalator to the top, I decided to fill her in.

"That girl. Her name's Elliana. She was asking me for scent recommendations, and we sort of just got into a conversation. I gave her my number so we can hang out sometime. She said she wanted to make some friends in the area."

"Dummy, she didn't want any recommendations. She was trying to socialize. It's the oldest scheme in the book," replied Mia.

"Or maybe she just needed help. Not everybody's like you."

"Okay, but did you actually see her take your advice?"

"No, but..." My voice trailed off.

"Exactly. No buts," she interrupted.

Our conversation was short-lived as we finally arrived outside of the clothing store. It had a distinctly different vibe from the perfume shop. Bright neon lights framed the windows and doorways, contrasting the black exterior. Meanwhile, the inside was a hot pink paradise and consisted of retro t-shirts and blinged-out crop tops. Strong smells of vanilla gave the room a rather bold atmosphere, a feeling that my sister emitted on a daily basis. I could see why she liked this place so much.

Immediately, Mia rushed over to the new arrivals and eyed a plethora of trendy shirts: a pink crop top covered in white hearts, a black and white checkered jacket, an ugly yellow sweatshirt, and a hot pink tee with an image of a distorted smile. She grabbed all that she could, practically juggling each item in her hands.

"Maybe you should put some stuff back," I suggested.

"No, I need to try them all. I mean, what if I looked amazing in *this*?" she asked, holding up another tee over her outfit.

"I think you'd look more amazing without balancing all of those clothes."

"Whatever. I'm going to the dressing room to try them on," she protested.

I simply sighed and shook my head. A woman shopping next to me saw our interaction and laughed.

"I know how it is. I have a teenage daughter who acts just like that. She's in the changing room right now," she said.

"Yeah well, that's teenagers for you," I responded. "If you don't mind me asking, what's your daughter's name?"

"It's Meilin. She just turned fourteen."

"Well, maybe she'd get along with my sister." I laughed.

After a few minutes, a young girl I assumed to be the woman's daughter returned from the dressing room and walked out of the store with her mother. I bid her farewell as she left, slightly disappointed that Mia had taken her sweet time. But that was Mia for you. We could be running an hour late, yet she would still be getting ready in the bathroom. Nothing made her hurry. When we'd cross the street, I'd always be as courteous as I could, lightly jogging on the road. Meanwhile, my sister would lag behind, her eyes buried in her phone as she walked.

I snapped my attention back to reality and realized that Mia still hadn't returned. Only one other person was shopping in the store, so I took the time to enjoy the quiet. A soft ring of pop music played from an overhead speaker, further adding to the spunky atmosphere. People conversed outside at café tables, happily sipping caffeinated drinks and typing away on laptops. Children begged their mothers to take them to the toy stores, the ones that flashed vibrant rainbow colors.

It was the type of feeling that only busy malls could produce. I had always found solace in the feeling, in the abundance of happiness. Maybe that's why I agreed to come here so often, whether I purchased something or not. Maybe it wasn't my sister's bribes or complaints, but simply the touch of joy I felt when visiting. Especially during the holidays, when festive lights would twinkle and shine, and the merry laughs of people of all ages rang in my ears. It allowed me to experience an absence of stress, at least for a short time, as I browsed the catalogs of brands and products.

I hadn't come here in a while since life got too complicated too fast, and I suddenly came to the realization that things were about to go downhill. No more frequent mall visits. No more enjoying the weekends with friends or hanging out after school. I never got a break. And I knew that as soon as I stepped foot into my house once again, fear would take over. When I was at the mall, I never wanted to go home. I *hated* home. The plastered blue walls, the wooden porch outside, the frosted glass windows. It made me sick. I could count every crack in the floors, every piece of trash in the garbage, every portrait on the mantle because, God help me, I was obsessed. I thought that if I memorized every little detail of every room, that I might just feel something toward that wretched place. But I didn't.

I returned my focus to the neon store in which I stood, waiting for my sister. Only about thirty minutes had passed, when in reality, it felt like hours. I tried to prepare a faux complaint for when she returned, just to get a rise out of her, but the buzz of conversations outside distracted me. I felt at peace once again, lost in the world of the mall.

Suddenly, in the midst of the happy shoppers and the light chatter of civilians, I heard it.

We all heard it.

Wiiiouuu. Wiiiouuu.

A dreadful siren. A high-pitched ring that vibrated within my ears. Goose bumps arose on my arms and legs. The mood in the air shifted. Looking outside the glass of the small store, blurs of people flickered within view, except they were screaming and shoving each other. This was no longer a mall. It was a war zone.

Wiiiouuu. Wiiiouuu.

"Please, I lost my son! Somebody, please help!" a young woman shouted to no one in particular, trying to get anyone's attention.

Mia came running out of the dressing room, still wearing a try-on outfit, the navy-blue tag clashing with the colors of the top. "Will somebody care to tell me what the hell is going on?"

Wiiiouuu. Wiiiouuu.

"There's a bomb in the building. You should get out of here," a woman yelled into the store.

With those words, it was as if life itself flipped upside down. Time froze. I could hear my heart beating. My legs went stiff. My blood ran cold. I felt as if in that moment, I could hear the bomb ticking away, counting down the seconds to my inevitable demise. The running stampede outside grew larger by the second. On instinct, I grabbed Mia's wrist and sprinted toward the entrance of the shop. We had no other option than to become one with the crowd. And so, I ran in synchrony with the strangers around me.

Left foot.

Right foot.

Heels clicked against heels on the hard tiled floors.

Left foot.

Right foot.

My body rocked back and forth from the constant shoving.

Left foot.

Right foot.

It was hard to move but I had to push forward. *Left foot, right foot,* I told myself. As I ran, the only thing I could think of was how badly I wanted to go home. I wanted to eat my mom's homemade ravioli. I wanted to hear my sister rant to me about school. So why? Why did I hate that place so much? Why would I *ever* want to be anywhere else than home?

My chest ached. My lungs yearned for air. My hands burned from gripping my sister so tightly. But none of that mattered now. We had one goal. *We had to escape.* With each step, my life flashed before my eyes. The first time I tried ice cream, Mia winning the National Talent Show, my dad teaching me how to ride a bike, all the way up until today. I had finally made a new friend, Elliana. Now she was probably getting slammed onto these cold mall floors by the raging stampede.

Knowing that the bomb could go off any moment now was just enough motivation to keep me going. It fueled my burning adrenaline. It gave me a purpose.

Left foot.

Right foot.

Mia pushed through behind me as I gave her a subtle over-the-shoulder glance. Her unbought t-shirt was still as prominent as ever. If we weren't in a dire situation, I would've been jealous of her because somehow, she still made running for her life look good.

"Hey, look at it this way. If we escape, you get a free shirt," I yelled over the commotion. I know it probably wasn't the most appropriate thing to say at that time, but we both needed a lighthearted joke.

She forced a smile. "Then let's hope we make it out alive."

Finally, we reached the escalator to the first floor. It had been disabled. Going down was a challenge with the swarm of people, yet I still held onto Mia.

Left foot.
Right foot.
Left foot.
Right foot.

I don't know what happened after that. We ran faster than ever on the ground level. The exit was just within our reach. My hands were sweating. My grasp on Mia loosened. The weight I was holding suddenly lightened. And before I knew it, she was gone. Lost in the crowd. I let go of my sister. I forced her into the sea of bodies. But I couldn't stop running. I couldn't yell out her name. I couldn't turn around. I had to keep moving, Mia or no Mia. My stomach wrenched, but there was no time to feel guilty. There was no time to look behind me. I was mentally paralyzed with fear, unable to stop myself. My survival instincts kicked in. I was on autopilot. I sucked up my impending tears and hoped for the best, that she was still okay. I blocked out the possibility that she had fallen, gotten crushed by the feet of those who fled in fear. I didn't know. I didn't want to know. I didn't want to know anything. I just wanted to get out. To survive.

Finally, I saw the exit in front of me.

"One at a time please, one at a time!" Security guards and police stopped the flow of traffic, making people file out in pairs.

I was right there. I could see the light pouring in from outside. I heard ambulances in the parking lot.

Left foot.

Right foot.

Left foot.

Right foot.

My escape was right there.

Boom.

All I saw was a flash, and then I collapsed to the ground. Flying debris hit me in the head, and warm blood rushed down my back. A burning sensation of death washed over me. I let myself give up. I surrendered to the feeling. My last thoughts were of my home, my sister, my mom. My final thoughts. My last memories.

And then, *I felt myself die.*

CHAPTER 2

I opened my eyes to the white walls of a large industrial office building. It reeked of cheap paint and rusted metal, and some of the light fixtures had been abused. The colors weren't remarkably diverse either. Sad shades of blue, gray, and white adorned every appliance and piece of furniture. For some reason, I couldn't remember how I got there or what my name was. It was a frustrating sensation, knowing so little, if I even recalled what frustration felt like. My head danced in circles around the room as I tried to associate with something, *anything*, that would make a lightbulb go off. Nothing.

The sound of ticking inched closer in my mind, taunting me, counting each second, I spent in this awful building. All the while, an ever so familiar beeping disoriented me in my lethargic state. My hair and clothes were completely clean, and I wore a strange white shirt with navy blue sweats. Checking to see if there was anything recognizable, I slipped my hands into my pockets and rummaged through them to find something that could help me remember my identity or give me any indication of where I was. To my dismay, the only thing I came across was a singular ticket. It had a crinkle cut design along the edges, and in dark blue text read "CHECK-IN CERTIFICATION, #071608." I didn't know how I got it, what the numbers meant, or what the check-in was. I didn't know anything. There were a few other people around me. All looked oddly familiar, but I couldn't put my finger on where I had seen them before.

Suddenly, as my vision became clearer and the dizzying sensation in my head ceased, I realized that I was moving. A handful of people were moving with me on a conveyer belt that transported us across a facility. Looking ahead, it seemed to stretch on forever. Yet somehow, that was the least of my concerns. As I watched the people on the transporter beside me, something seemed very off. We were all wearing the same white polo shirt, like in some twisted institution. But most importantly, everyone had the same tickets in hand.

I turned around and looked at a younger girl behind me. She had short, bowl-shaped black hair and icy blue eyes. Her expression was blank, as if this were just any other occasion, so I figured she might know what was going on.

"Excuse me, do you know where we are and why we have these tickets?" I asked.

The girl ignored me and walked ahead on the conveyer belt. She didn't say a word but rather stuck her snobby nose in the air and continued walking.

Behind her, taking her spot, was another young girl, one with light brown hair and a freckled face. She looked a bit disturbed and, panic clear in her movements, gently leaned over and whispered in my ear, "Don't question anything here. Just give the workers at HQ your ticket and pretend like everything is normal." She pointed up ahead, and I saw a militarized woman with a blue uniform poised by a sign that read "Headquarters." As the other kids reached the check-in area, employees scanned their tickets and assigned them a colored wristband.

"Oh, thanks. By the way, what's your name?" I asked, examining the girl's freckles. "You seem very familiar."

"I don't know. None of us do."

And suddenly, it dawned on me what little information I truly had. The last thing I remembered was a flash of light and a weird stinging sensation throughout my body. For some reason, there was a strange emptiness inside me, an out-of-place feeling. I had a name, I was a person, I think I had a younger sister, but whenever I tried to figure out the "who," my mind drew a blank. I suppose my mind had drawn many blanks. But if everyone here was in the same boat as I was, why weren't *they* freaking out? Was I the only one curious as to how I got here, or who I was? With an abundance of confusing questions, I turned to face the brunette who stood behind me.

"Why was that other girl so rude to me? I didn't say anything wrong," I stated matter-of-factly.

"She's probably in shock. Same with everyone else here."

"You're not in shock."

"No, not anymore."

And with that, she walked ahead of me to hand in her ticket. If anything, my interaction with her only made the situation more confusing. Her face looked so recognizable. It definitely didn't feel like the first time we had met.

Looking ahead, I saw the check-in center. The other kids gave a worker their ticket and, in return, gained a colored wristband. From there, they dispersed into distinct groups. All of the workers, however, looked weirdly out of place. They wore blue jumpsuits with name tags attached to the front, and around their waists, they carried belt bags.

As I reached the entrance to Headquarters, I stepped up and gave the nearest receptionist my ticket. She scanned it and then looked at me with an odd smile.

"So, just for verification purposes, would you please state your full name and age?" she asked, a hint of malevolence present in her voice.

I did a double take and stood there like a deer in the headlights, unable to move or think. *Unable to remember.*

"Sorry, I... I'm ... not quite sure," I dumbly stuttered.

I was expecting worse. So much worse. They would think I was a liar, a trespasser, possibly even get security to take me away. But instead, the woman just smiled and nodded. "No worries, dear. We can get that issue all fixed up for you after your induction."

She reached into a compartment on her desk and pulled out a red pass. "Go to the Waiting Room, sector A1. Announcements will begin shortly." I took the slip and observed its delicate details. Then she took out a red wristband and secured it around my hand. "Good luck! We hope you enjoy your forty-day stay!"

I was quickly ushered out of the line, still unable to process everything that had recently happened to me. This *place* appeared to be an office or a facility of sorts. Everyone was unified. Everyone followed the rules. But yet something was amiss. It felt like the workers had a secret—as if they were hiding something from us, and I couldn't pinpoint exactly what it was. The woman at the check-in seemed suspiciously vague. "We hope you enjoy your forty-day stay!" Those were her exact words. What was a "forty-day stay"? And more importantly, what was going to happen after those forty days were over? Even if I did have a place to return to, I surely didn't remember that place now. This was my new *home*. Or at least what I imagined a home to be.

Behind the rows of check-in lines, I could see a vast array of rooms and offices. I thought this place was big before, but man, was I mistaken. From my perspective, it looked like a futuristic mall. The center of the lobby was filled with chatting kids and glass, booth-shaped structures. Each booth was equipped with gadgets such as touchscreen TVs and smartphones that looked as if they were being used for filling out surveys and wellness checks. Toward the back of the facility was a cafeteria. Metal tables and chairs stretched out in rows throughout the room while a place for preparing food was stationed beside them. Toward the left and right walls of the lobby were sectors, categorized stations for attending to different needs. They seemed to go on forever, with signs above each room containing a letter and a number. One of the rooms, however, was locked and guarded by security. It was A-0.5, and it didn't seem like one of the ordinary sectors. The two men standing watch wore vicious scowls, contrasting with the rather neutral look most of the other workers had. They were armed, and instead of wearing blue jumpsuits, sported protective vests and gear.

I scanned each aisle, watching as synchronized children swiftly checked in and out of different sectors. Finally, I landed upon A1, my stop.

A1 was marked with a dark red symbol and had the label "Waiting Room" plastered across the top of the doorway. The moment I stepped inside, I knew that there was no going back. I also suspected that I wouldn't be getting many answers here either. I noted the busy workers, each situated at desks spaced around the room, which currently housed about a handful of other kids in chairs lined up against the walls. The workers all had that same hypnotic, yet threatening aura, with no intention of letting me leave. They were very hushed and working diligently.

I sat on an empty chair near the entrance where the other kids were waiting for the supposed induction, trying to get some sort of reassurance, some sort of clarity. A girl with red hair and round circular glasses fidgeted with a few loose rings on her fingers. Meanwhile, a boy sitting next to her held a stack of papers in his hands, intently scribbling in the margins with a navy-blue pen while reading over the lines of text. I wanted to ask him how he got the paper and pen, but I was afraid of receiving the silent treatment again. So instead, I decided to take in my surroundings. Although the facility seemed well put together, looking closer, I noticed all of the small imperfections and details, counting the number of cracks on the walls or chips of paint on the floor.

I swayed my feet back and forth as they dangled over the edge of the metal chair, and again, that familiar ticking noise rose in my ears—mocking me, teasing me, counting all the meaningless seconds I spent in this room. I became increasingly impatient, waiting for something, anything to happen—something that could give me purpose or something that could give me answers. But alas, answers weren't in my immediate future.

Eventually, after mindlessly sitting around for some time, an announcement came through from an overhead speaker. "Attention all new guests, please report to the Auditorium, sector A2, for your induction." The voice sounded gravelly and hoarse as a result of the mediocre quality of the speaker. All at once, the kids began to shuffle out of the Waiting Room and made their way to the Auditorium.

Sector A2 was a much larger area in comparison to sector A1. The roof and walls curved where they met, creating a dome shape. A stage was centered at the end of the building, surrounded by metallic chairs. Workers instructed us to find a seat, so I made myself comfy in the back row, not wanting any attention on me. As I watched each kid file through the line of chairs, I realized how few people there actually were. The Auditorium was more like a barren wasteland.

The fluorescent lights in the room dimmed as a woman wearing a blue and white suit stood up on the stage. Her blonde hair was wound tightly in an obnoxious bun while the fakest of smiles spread across her face.

"Hello, everybody. I am Margret, one of the co-owners of this operation. I am here today to tell you all about how this facility works. My main goal is to make you feel at home, so please do not be scared." Her voice was almost as obnoxious as her hairstyle. "First, let me begin with why you are here. I know you must be awfully confused. Just know that you were brought here for a reason, and after forty days, your visit will be over. The time goes by faster than you may think!"

So that's why it's called a forty-day stay. I comply with their rules, adapt to their customs without question, and after forty days, I'll be out of here?

"All of you will be given a schedule that outlines your day-to-day activities," she began. "You will be required to take certain courses throughout your time here such as *Anatomy Training, Computing, Geometry*, and *Hypnosis Studies*. You will also have the option to take elective classes during your free hours or as a substitute for one of the subjects listed. Sign-up sheets for other specific courses will be located in sector C7. Each day, there will be an hour for breakfast, lunch-time, and dinnertime. The menu changes often, so please refrain from complaints. Breakfast begins at eleven, lunch at two, and dinner at five.

"After dinner, there will be two hours of study hall called Common Hour. These hours will be used for catching up on work, fulfilling needed duties, visiting other dorms, et cetera. That being said, everybody must be back in their rooms by eight o'clock sharp. There will be consequences for roaming during After Hours." Margret paused to take a deep breath before resuming her speech.

"Now, let's review the rules of this facility. Failure to follow the rules will result in a serious punishment. One—be on time for all your classes. Two—pass each class with 70% or higher. Three—do not share your identity with others. Four—respect the workers. Five—do as we say. Six—never go into sector A-0.5. That area is strictly forbidden. And seven—do not question anything."

The room fell completely silent. No fidgeting with rings or scribbling on papers. No coughing or sneezing. Just pure silence. The woman on the stage clicked her tongue and continued to smile. She didn't even look human.

"Anyway, now that we got that out of the way. If you haven't already, please pick up a green pass and make your way to sector B9, the Observations Room. You will be given a guide who will ask you some quick questions and provide you with a written schedule of all of your classes and events. They will also lead you to your dormitory, where you will be paired with a roommate for the next forty days."

All of the kids, including me, got up from their seats and made their way out of the Auditorium, picking up their green passes as they left. The Observations Room didn't sound too pleasing. I was a bit more relaxed now that I was getting a set routine, but my mind still throbbed with unanswered questions. Yet again, nobody felt the need to tell us how we got here or what we were doing prior to being forced into this place. I also knew that now I'd have to interact with even more of the unsettling workers.

On my way to B9, I analyzed something Margret had said during her announcements. "Failure to follow the rules will result in a serious punishment." What was a serious punishment? You'd think after all the effort they put into enforcing these rules, they would at least have the courtesy to elaborate a bit more. Unless, of course, they couldn't. I wondered if it had something to do with sector A-0.5. Maybe that was the big secret they were hiding. Maybe, just behind those doors, were the answers to the unknown, the reason I was here now, wandering these halls.

After scanning the aisles and walking down the lobby, I landed upon B9. It was color coded light green and had the title "Observations Room" on the top of the doors. There I stood, knowing nothing about who I was, just wishing, *hoping* that I would leave this room with answers—anything to make me feel like a person again. As I stepped through the entrance and observed the plethora of computers and high-tech gadgets, I knew that this party was just getting started, and it wasn't going to end anytime soon. I was stuck here for the next forty days.

CHAPTER 3

The Observations Room looked very advanced. Projectors and holograms were stationed in different areas, along with various machines. In one corner, scientific tools lay scattered across tabletops as workers wearing white scrubs ran tests on various substances. Meanwhile, opposite of that, researchers sporting blue jumpsuits scribbled away on notepads, typing data into their computers. I wasn't quite sure where to go as everybody looked so engrossed in their work. Technological manifestations and artificial intelligence made the room a beacon of life and invention. Eventually, after staring for a while, I noticed a line of kids waiting for further instructions. I made my way to the back of the queue and anticipated what would come next.

As I emerged at the front of the line, I was greeted by a rigid woman with soft features. She appeared stoic—robot-like, with cold eyes and a phony smile spread across her face, like a humanoid Cheshire cat, and a blue uniform with a name tag that read "Theresa: Guide."

"Hello there! My name is Theresa." She pointed to the tag. "And I will be assisting you as you get set up in our facility. I know you have a lot of questions, but so do I, and it is your job to answer them. Think you can do that for me?" Her voice sounded like nails on a chalkboard. It had a disgusting amount of faux cheeriness and stretched out syllables, and she spoke to me as if I were a baby. Despite my not being much shorter than she was, she crouched down to meet me at eye level. Her breath smelled minty as she chewed hard on her gum.

I simply nodded in response, not wanting to engage.

"Perfect. Come with me!"

Begrudgingly, I followed Theresa across the room, where she led me behind the experimenters and into an office that stood hidden in the back. The secret area was home to a large beige desk with a tablet and clipboard placed in the middle. It was quite dim—the only light source was a single fluorescent lamp. I sauntered over to the far side of the table and took a seat across from her. Meanwhile, Theresa powered on a tablet and grabbed a dark blue stylus from one of her pockets and tapped away at a few buttons on the screen. The device had a navy case with four random numbers at the top, along with the letters "MLD" and some mysterious symbols. The buzzing of sound effects rang from the speakers as an occasional popping noise slowly became audible. Then, as the device lit up a bright orange, she repositioned herself in the chair and began asking me questions.

"This is a general questions survey. Please answer every item honestly. Failure to comply will result in serious punishment."

There it is again: serious punishment.

"Question one: what is your favorite color?"

I let out an annoyed chuckle and cocked my head in confusion. These people, these *workers,* brought me all the way to their facility, dragged me into an "induction," and brought me for testing in some sad, beige office just to ask me my favorite color? After all the trouble and impatience, all the whirring of questions I had myself, the most important piece of information they could gather from me was seriously none other than my *favorite damn color?*

"What exactly is the point of this?" I asked, crossing my arms in defiance.

Theresa's demeanor switched from fake and bubbly to extremely bitter in a matter of seconds. "Excuse me, but I'm asking the questions—not you."

"So, you ask me what my favorite color is? If you're trying to get some crucial information from me, I don't think that's going to help you very much."

She lightly slammed the tablet on the table, still giving me that stupid smile. "Please hurry up and answer the question. There is a line of people outside waiting to be assessed, and I do not have the time for resistance."

Her abrupt change in attitude startled me, yet the urge to leap across the desk and punch that stupid grin off of her face was strong. "Yellow. It's yellow."

But I knew that wasn't true. I couldn't explain why, but something inside me told me that I hated the color yellow.

"See, it wasn't that hard, now was it?" She entered my response into the device and moved onto the next question. "Question two: what is your favorite breakfast food?"

I stared down at my hands in defeat. Silence did me no good, and I knew that eventually, I would have to follow the rules. Just as I was about to say that I wasn't a fan of breakfast, something within me changed. Strange sensations made my brain tingle while my vision fogged up with colors and images. As I closed my eyes, the world around me transformed, and a hazy scene entered my memory…

A young girl with her back facing me. I was in the kitchen, and she was hunched over a stove flipping pancakes. On a table stood a jar of maple syrup and a small tray of blueberries.

"Get ready to have a breakfast like no other," she said.

Then she turned to face me…

I broke out of the trance and noticed that I was still in the dimly lit office. That girl in my mind had disappeared before I could tell what was going on. I never got to see her face, but just hearing her voice, being in her presence, made me feel comforted, almost like I was right at home.

"Hello? Are you paying attention?" Theresa's voice snapped me back into my harsh reality.

"Sorry. I guess it's … pancakes?" I answered. I could never recall having them, but after seeing that strange vision, it felt like the right thing to say.

"Alright, pancakes it is!" She documented my response once again and continued reading the list of questions, but I was just too distracted. My mind still raced from the previous vision-like daze. It felt like I had known that girl for forever, but upon coming back to my senses, my memory was completely wiped of her visage. The kitchen smelled of fresh food. I felt happy. All I did know for sure was that wherever that was, it was better than this place.

Suddenly, in the midst of the questions, I came to a realization: What if I had it twisted? What if that vision was my real life, and everything going on in this facility was just a figment of my imagination? That would mean that I wasn't bound by these rules, that I didn't have to answer anything. There would be no consequences or severe punishments. I'd be in charge.

"Question three: how old are you?"

I kept my mouth shut, staring Theresa right in the eyes.

"It's okay if you're not sure. Just answer to the best of your ability," she reassured.

"I don't need to play your games anymore, Theresa."

She looked at me in disbelief, her smile wiped clean.

Point one for me.

"This is, in fact, not a game, but a professional survey. Your cooperation is needed."

"How about *you* cooperate? From now on, you'll listen to everything I tell you to do."

"This will be your last warning. Please answer the question." Her voice was stern as there was no more façade masking her words and actions.

My patience was a ticking time bomb, and the clock finally got down to zero. I felt the walls around us shrink as I stared at the woman across from me. Her brows were furrowed, accentuating the fine wrinkles on her forehead while her eyes felt like they could burn right through my soul. The only sound I heard was the beating of my own heart as it seemed to echo throughout the vast emptiness of the room. I glanced at the tablet in Theresa's hand. The glowing screen illuminated the dark space between us as I observed the upside-down text. I hated these questions. I hated this place. And I wanted them to know it.

In the blink of an eye, I lunged across the desk. My leg kicked the chair back as I exerted my force onto the table. Theresa couldn't react in time. I snatched the tablet from her hands and slammed it on the floor. But that wasn't enough. I stomped on the case as it lay face down on the ground, the sound of cracking glass like music to my ears.

Left foot.

Right foot.

I repeatedly stepped on it over and over. I wanted to rid that device of any questions it had for me. Theresa yelled, but I ignored her.

Left foot.

Right foot.

My body jolted backward from a sudden touch. Theresa grabbed my shoulders and violently spun me around, pinning me down on the table. I attempted to escape her grasp but didn't get very far. She had me in a tough grip. And with one swift movement, she reached into the bag strapped around her waist and pulled out a tranquilizer gun.

"Answer the question next time."

The last thing I heard was the trigger pop as the gun was aimed at my chest. A flash of white light blinded me and rocked my bones with an electrifying jolt. It felt like my skin was ripping apart, melting under the pressure of the sudden blast. I was falling down a tunnel of no return, descending deeper and deeper into the heart of the magnetizing energy. I couldn't even hear my own screams. I was gone.

"What should I do?"

"Well, you pretend it never happened, that's what. The darts are just a behavioral precaution, so I say you grab a new device and sit right back down in that chair. Nothing worth losing your job over."

When I opened my eyes, I was back inside the dim office. Theresa sat at the table across from me, smiling once again as the navy tablet rested perfectly in her hands.

I didn't understand. I remembered lunging across the desk and smashing the tablet that she was holding into fragmented bits. It was so very fresh in my mind. Then she shot me with a tranquilizer dart, I was pinned and helpless on the table, and

I heard voices talking. I remembered it all so clearly as the events replayed on a loop in my mind. So why was she still smiling? Why was she holding the device that I had destroyed?

Theresa's voice broke me out of my daze. "Question two: what is your favorite breakfast food?"

I froze in my seat. Goosebumps appeared on my arms as I pieced everything together. I already answered her favorite breakfast food question! I was sure of it!

"It's pancakes. I thought you knew?" I answered.

"Well, how would I know if you weren't here to tell me?" She smiled and moved on to the next question. "Number three…"

"How old are you? You don't have to tell me that one," I cut her off, knowing that was the next on the list. But that was impossible! How could I know that?

"Yes, that's correct! How did you know I was going to ask you that?"

My voice went quiet. "A lucky guess, I suppose," I replied, lying through my teeth.

Trying to focus on the rest of the survey was difficult. When she hit me with the tranquilizer dart, I experienced a familiar sensation. It was the same way I felt when I first entered the facility—the feeling of not remembering anything. However, the effects seemed less extreme now. As I tried to recall my memories, I realized I couldn't exactly make out certain thoughts. Everything was vague, like my confusion upon first waking up here. It was almost like I was hit with a wave of brain fog.

Theresa continued to ask more questions such as, "What grade are you going into? What school do you attend? What is the last thing you remember?" I didn't have an answer to any of them. My mind was devoid of all memories, all thoughts. I simply felt like a shell of my former self—whoever *that* was.

All the while, Theresa continued to press buttons on her tablet, sending all my responses to the supposed people in charge.

Finally, the last question of the test gave me a strange uneasiness.

"Who are you?"

The question jolted me. Three simple words that, in any normal circumstance, should have been easily answered. My name. My heritage. My personality. Wants. Likes. Needs. Desires… all of what made me *me* wrapped up and unidentified in that one question. The fact that I could not even respond with a name was infuriating. How badly I wanted to scream at the top of my lungs! Between the words of that question and the spaces of that spoken sentence were the answers to everything I needed and wanted to know about *me*. My appearance, my blood ties, my age, my experiences, and how I somehow wound up in this place. Unfortunately, my memories were wiped clean upon entering, but I knew I wasn't crazy. I knew that I had lived before. I just didn't know *how*.

I fidgeted in my chair for a few seconds, thinking intently about the question…

Who am I?

"Sorry, I… I don't know."

Theresa flashed me her signature smile before typing away on the tablet screen once again. A few more taps on the device and an extra toothy grin indicated that I was finally done. "Great! Your survey is complete! Welcome home, Stella."

Stella.

The name echoed in my ears with a familiar ring. Theresa pulled up a portfolio on the tablet and slid it in my direction. At the top, the name read "Stella Winterfield" in bold text and listed many physical attributes around the screen—dirty blonde hair, blue eyes, seventeen years old, 115 pounds, 5'3". It also included other bits of information such as *had one sibling, attended Haven Crest Highschool, worked at a local retail store part time, father deceased, mother widowed.* I scanned the bullet points and read each item carefully. Forgotten details about my life were unfolding in front of my very eyes, yet they were merely words with no concrete memory attached to them. I read the words as if I were reading the biography of a stranger.

Theresa then handed me a written report of my daily schedule, thus confirming my stay at the facility. Breakfast began at 11:00 am and continued for an hour. My first two classes of the morning were Geometry and Anatomy Training. Then I had an hour lunch, and the rest of the day was occupied with my remaining classes, Hypnosis Studies and Computing. Dinner was at 5:00 pm, and everyone was given a designated time for Common Hour. The curfew to be back at the dorms was no later than 8:00 pm.

"Now that you've reviewed your itinerary, let's get you all set up, shall we?" Theresa chirped in a sing-song voice.

I honestly did not want to have any more interactions with this woman, but since she was my so-called guide, I had no other option.

"First, let me go over a few rules. I know that you're excited about learning your name, but you must never use it anywhere outside of this room. Others must not know about your identity. Instead, you will be referred to as 'Forty-Eight.' Am I clear?"

"Yes, ma'am," I dryly replied.

"Great! Your new uniforms will be shipped to your dorm this evening. It will be a set of white tees and button-up shirts with your number on the back so people can easily identify you. It's required that you wear the uniforms every day," she said while collecting loose sheets of paper from the desk. "For our next part of the tour, allow me to show you around our facility so you can become familiar with the layout." Theresa got up from her chair and motioned for me to follow her outside. Finally, I was escaping this wretched beige office.

We walked out of The Observations Room and arrived at the lobby where she proceeded to give me an overview of the different sectors and areas. From what I could tell, this was all some sort of laboratory built to run their grand experiments. The workers tested out different "-ologies" of science—biology, psychology, et cetera. But for what reason, I couldn't tell. I also didn't know how this related to me in any way. If I came here for a reason, it's not like my hazy memory would be of much use in their experiments.

As the tour of Headquarters continued, an alarm sounded, followed by menacing shouts. The high and low rising pitch of the siren was so familiar, but I couldn't tell why. Men in protective armor and face masks formed a single file line down the aisles, demanding that people move out of their way. The halls shone a bright red from the flash of the alarm systems while screams could be heard in the distance.

A muffled sound came from Theresa's bag of items. "Attention everyone, this is a code yellow. I repeat, this is a code yellow. Please act accordingly." The man's voice sounded robotic and grainy as a result of the static.

"Excuse me, but what's going on?" I asked, slightly concerned. The scene was all too real, like I'd lived through it before.

"There's been an attempted escape. It's when some awfully behaved students think that it's a good idea to try to run away. They always get caught in the end," she responded.

As if on cue, the armed men returned holding a young boy in handcuffs and brought him into sector X2 at the very end of the hall. I recognized him from earlier in the Waiting Room.

He had been the one preoccupied with taking notes on a stack of papers, scribbling within the margins.

"What will they do with him?" I asked.

"Let's hope you never have to find out."

The lights went back to normal, and Theresa resumed the tour as if nothing had happened. She appeared to not care about the situation, and judging by the way she merely scoffed and walked along, I supposed incidents like these happened often.

Paying attention to the rest of the tour was difficult as the sight of the boy with the anxious face getting dragged along by security was permanently engraved in my mind.

"Now, for our last and final stop, let me show you to your dorm! This will be your shared living space for the next forty days. It is past dinnertime, so we will provide you with a complimentary meal to eat in your room," she said, leading the way to a new sector.

The top of the room was labeled "Dormitory 15" and color coded in bright yellow.

"Unfortunately, this is where our tour ends. If you need any assistance, please report to sector A5. It was nice meeting you, Forty-Eight!" With that, Theresa walked away, leaving me standing in front of my dorm.

I looked at the yellow trimming on the doorframe and, with one push of the handle, took a deep breath and braced myself for what was to come inside. After all, *this was my new home*.

CHAPTER 4

As I stepped inside my quarters, I could confidently say that this one was pleasant. A humble kitchen was on the left side of the room, featuring a microwave and mini freezer, along with a table and set of chairs. On the right side was a desk that had numerous cabinets and compartments, paired with a comfy blue couch to match the décor. Toward the back of the room was a grand bunkbed adorned with pristine white bedsheets and blue pillows. A bookshelf and nightstand were beside it with multiple books and a telephone in the center. However, I suspected that the phone was more of an intercom system that connected our room with the other sectors.

Around the corner of the common living area was a small bathroom. It had ocean blue walls and a frosted glass shower with white curtains. Small soaps that smelled of lavender and honey were neatly placed in dishes by the sinks. There was also a mirror, and for the first time in a long time, I was able to *see* myself.

I stepped out into the living room and crashed on the bottom bunk face-first. I was so exhausted that I knew the moment I shut my eyes, I would drift off into a deep sleep. The bedding was soft and allowed for my body to sink comfortably into the mattress. Everything seemed perfect.

Suddenly, I heard the distinct sound of a door being opened. A bright light crept into the room and washed away the orange fluorescent hues of the dorm. The shuffling sounds of feet made their way inside, and I stood up and turned my body to face who had entered. To my dismay, it wasn't just any random person.

Her striking black bowl-cut stood out like a sore thumb, and her icy blue eyes pierced right into my soul. My mood shifted upon seeing who my new roommate was—the snobby face I wished I'd never see again. It was the same girl who ignored me on the conveyer belt and walked away with a look of disgust. It was like hate at first sight.

"I got your dinner. Come sit," she said, a bit more demanding than welcoming, as she tossed a plate of wrapped frozen food on the table.

In a black plastic container was my microwavable meal. It was a tray of peas and corn along with barbeque chicken and a selection of different sauces. She put her dish in the microwave and took out two bottles of water from the fridge.

The scent of vegetables and chicken wafted through the air as she grabbed her heated portion and set it down on the table. I took my turn at the microwave and gave myself a napkin, lightly placing it under the frozen water which was still damp from the condensation.

"So, what number did you get?" she asked right as my food finished cooking. "You know, since we can't say our names."

"Forty-Eight," I bitterly replied, not interested in the attempt at conversing.

"I'm Fifty."

I sat down at the table, and we ate in silence, occasionally giving each other subtle glares between bites. There was an uncomfortable tension between us that made the feeling in the room very awkward.

"By the way, I'm calling the top bunk," she announced.

I became increasingly annoyed with every word she spoke. "Whatever. I'm fine with the bottom."

I quickly scarfed down the rest of my meal and threw the plastic tray into a nearby trash bin. I didn't know how late it was, and I honestly didn't care. All I wanted to do was enjoy the peaceful bliss of sleep. I trudged over to my bed, not caring to change out of my dirty clothes. As soon as my head hit the plush pillow of the bottom bunk, I was out like a light and slipped away into a sea of unconsciousness.

39 DAYS REMAINING

Brrrmm. Brrrmm.

My eyes flicked open from a loud suctioning sound; I was still disoriented from last night's slumber.

Brrrmm. Brrrmm.

As I observed the surroundings of the dorm, my vision slowly returned. Fifty vigorously vacuumed the rug. The sound unsettled my insides as it reverberated throughout the room.

"What the hell are you doing?" I yelled above the noise. She didn't hear me and continued to vacuum.

"Hey! Bowl-cut! I said what the hell are you doing?" I repeated, louder this time.

She abruptly turned off the machine and looked at me with an annoyed gaze. "What does it look like I'm doing? Use some context clues to figure it out."

I ignored her comment and continued interrogating her, "What time is it anyway?" I asked. The windows beamed with sunlight, signaling the start of a new day.

"It's six. Now if that's too early for you, you can get your lazy ass back in bed and let me do the work around here," she snapped.

"Care to explain why you need to vacuum at six in the morning? Breakfast doesn't start for another five hours. Where did you even get that thing?"

"I'm being productive. If you had done the same, you would've seen that there's a closet in the back with cleaning supplies. Now leave me alone."

With that, she turned the vacuum back on and resumed her round of tidying. By now, I was far too awake to go back to sleep, so I decided to get up and get ready for my first official day of classes.

My uniforms had arrived during the night and were neatly stacked alongside my bed. Pairs of white shirts with "Forty-Eight" labeled on each back, as well as blue sweatpants, were neatly folded in a pile. I grabbed a set of clothes and made my way to the bathroom, grunting with each step.

The thought of a nice, warm shower brought a smile to my face—I was filthy, inside and out, and I knew a shower would help wake me up and get me feeling clean and somewhat like myself.

Whoever *that* was.

The water felt luxurious as it ran down my back. The compact bathroom quickly filled with steam, and I was immersed in the peaceful ambience of the shower as the aromas of honey and fresh flowers piqued my senses. Closing my eyes, I became truly lost in the tranquility of the room. But suddenly, the water ran cold, and the atmosphere shifted. My mind pounded as the world around me transformed into something different, something new.

I opened my eyes and saw a familiar blue house. It was dark and muggy as the rain poured down on my unprotected frame. Begrudgingly, I made my way to the front porch, admiring the wooden bench outside.

Knock. Knock. Knock

Three knocks, all in rapid succession. I needed to get inside as I was starting to catch a cold.

"Stella? Is that you? Where have you been?" An older woman spoke from inside the house.

I heard the door unlock as it began to open, the hinges slowly creaking. Finally, just before revealing who was on the other side, the scene disappeared in a flash.

I was back in the shower, as if nothing had happened. Another vision, but this time it felt more intense. I was eager to see who was on the other side of the door. Although I didn't exactly know what I was looking at, it all seemed very familiar—the mailbox, the blue plaster walls, the wooden bench, like I had been there before.

I stepped out of the shower, the sense of peace gone from the room, and put on my new uniform. I decided to make myself comfortable within the space by browsing through the cabinets. They contained miscellaneous bathroom items such as soaps, toothbrushes, toothpastes, and floss. Picking up a few tools, I decided to clean my teeth and brush out my hair. The sound of vacuuming outside was gone and instead replaced with intense rummaging. Boxes, bags, and papers of all kinds were being thrown around—another deep cleaning session by my roommate.

Once I looked presentable, I stepped out of the bathroom and back to the common area. Fifty scavenged through the desk drawers, organizing different compartments and making a greater mess than there was before.

There were still a good three hours before breakfast started, so I decided to peruse the bookshelves and find something interesting to read to pass the time. I stumbled upon a large purple book with gold edges and a fantastic dragon with black wings on the cover. It looked lengthy and interesting, the perfect thing to get me through the morning and survive another few hours with Fifty.

Ten minutes before breakfast, she finally stopped cleaning. "Get your ass up. We have to go," she commanded.

"Wow, I didn't even realize how fast the time went," I said.

"Sure. Now c'mon."

And just like that, we were out the door, about to begin our first day.

Fifty walked in slow strides throughout the lobby, her nose stuck up in the air. Words couldn't describe how much I disliked her. She was inconsiderate and entitled, speaking with minimal words and ending her sentences with small grunts or scoffs. Just as my new life in the facility seemed to start looking up, she had appeared. She was like a thunderstorm on a good day or a cookie filled with raisins, all the things that made my face contort in disgust. Her appearance was bold, even while wearing the standard uniforms. Those piercing blue eyes contrasted with her black head of hair. I couldn't stand it.

Finally, we arrived at the cafeteria. Comforting smells of fresh breakfast filled my nose with delight as other students made their way to the pick-up line. I quickly walked away from Fifty, not wanting to stand beside her any longer.

"If you miss curfew and get us both in trouble, I *will* kick your ass," she yelled, but her voice gradually faded in the distance among the sea of people.

I arrived at the meal line and saw trays of food spread out buffet style. They had everything. Scrambled, fried, and sunny-side-up eggs, pancakes, smoky sausages, bacon, yogurt… A worker wearing a white apron handed me a tray and allowed me to pick out a selection of food and drinks. I dug into the platters and grabbed some pancakes and eggs, along with a bottle of water. My stomach rumbled with impatience as I made my way over to an empty table.

I ate alone in silence but honestly didn't mind. I felt solace in the chatter and laughter of the people around me. Until suddenly, there was a light tap on my shoulder.

"Excuse me, may I sit here?" someone asked. It was none other than the freckled girl, the same person who had helped give me directions on the conveyer belt. I was glad to see her again.

"Of course," I replied.

Almost instantly, she sat beside me and struck up a conversation. "I'm Fifty-Seven. Nice to see you found your way around."

"It was all thanks to you. I'm Forty-Eight."

She smiled and gave a knowing nod. "By the way, would you like to take my extra food? I wasn't too hungry," she asked.

"Sure, I'm starving," I said, accepting her offer. She slid over the metal tray with ease, and my hand lightly brushed along the edges. After making contact with the dish, my vision became cloudy again and images manifested themselves in front of my eyes…

I was in a beautiful room. Lovely aromas filled my senses and made me feel at ease. I stared at my feet on the floor and grabbed ahold of my phone. A girl added her number into my contacts, listed under "Elliana."

"I'm new to the area, so I'm just getting to know people," *she stated.*

I looked up from the phone to meet her gaze, and everything disappeared in an instant.

"Hello? Forty-Eight? Earth to Forty-Eight," Fifty-Seven said, making quick snappy motions in front of my face. I had spaced out, staring at the metal tray. Yet again, there was another vision. The name *Elliana* rang in my head, although I couldn't remember who exactly Elliana was.

"Sorry, I'm just tired," I began.

"So, you saw it too?" Fifty-Seven abruptly cut me off.

"I'm sorry?"

"Those flashes of memories… like *visions*. It's been happening to me ever since I got here."

I sighed and continued eating. "It's probably just nothing. I wouldn't sweat it."

We sat in silence for a little bit, and I found myself tuning into the sounds of the people around me. The truth was the visions deeply worried me. They gave me a sense of unease and familiarity, despite not truly understanding them.

"This place is bad, you know," she said after a few minutes had gone by.

I dropped my fork and looked at her. Her eyes were glazed over ever so slightly.

"What do you mean?" I asked.

She paused and took a deep breath. "This is a *science* facility. These workers—they're treating us well as a way to 'feed' us— to make us better test subjects. The more you conform to their standards, the easier it is for them to manipulate you."

"How can you know for sure?" I asked.

"Are you seriously forgetting that they brought us here against our will and wiped all of our memories? We lived before this, and they just ripped our lives away from us. This place isn't nice at all. It's just one big façade. They shower you with food and lure you in with their hospitality, all while hiding behind closed doors and running tests on your DNA. It feels like a trap, doesn't it, Forty-Eight?"

I stared down at my feet, giving myself a chance to think. So far, I'd had a total of three visions. The first one was of a comforting blonde girl making breakfast in a kitchen. The second was of me standing in front of a blue house in the pouring rain. And finally, the third was of a girl named Elliana. What all three had in common was something I still didn't know. They were so vivid, like I'd lived there before. Deep down, somewhere in the pit of my stomach, I felt that Fifty-Seven was right, but I simply couldn't understand why. Why would scientists feel the need to kidnap children for some wacky experiments? But all things considered, I *had* seen and experienced some sketchy things here. During my survey with Theresa, I had memories of smashing the tablet and telling her off, right before getting hit with a strange dart and going from point A to point B in the matter of mere seconds. Not to mention the fact that grouping us into numbers or calling out "code yellows" struck me as suspicious.

"So, what happened to you?" I asked.

She shifted her body and turned in my direction. "If I told you, you wouldn't believe it."

"Try me."

"Alright, but don't say I didn't warn you," she began. "I remember something that happened before I got here. It was some sort of explosion. One minute I was eating, and the next, trying to escape from the ash and rubble. I found a girl, alive but barely breathing, and tried to save her, but it was too late.

All I could feel was death coursing through my veins. I can't describe it, but it was like my body shut down. The world went from burning orange flames of heat and fire to sudden darkness. I must have passed out."

She paused to collect her thoughts, then continued, "It didn't stop there though. I woke up surrounded by people in lab coats and jumpsuits, injecting me with different drugs. I was hooked up to machines, and all I could hear were their ominous whispers as they jotted down notes onto clipboards. But I did make out one piece of information. They said, 'It took her fifty minutes to cross.' Then all of a sudden, they noticed that I was awake and immediately covered my mouth with a cloth until I was out cold again. Those people were these very workers. Trust me when I say this, but they don't have your interests in mind."

"But then how come they've been telling us that we get to leave after forty-days? Kidnappers don't just let their hostages go."

Fifty-Seven remained silent with a grim expression on her face. Her demeanor quickly changed within seconds.

"Hey, answer my question. Why would they say they're letting us go? What happens after the forty-days are over?" I asked her again.

Silence.

"I know you can hear me. What happens after the forty-days are over?"

Silence.

"Answer, dammit! What's going to happen to us after forty-days?!"

My body shook. It was hard to breathe. The air around me was suffocating. I watched as Fifty-Seven's lip trembled. Her silence was killing me. I was scared.

"Forty-Eight, I think we die."

CHAPTER
UNKNOWN: PART 1

KATHERINE JONES

Katherine Jones had locks of brown hair which gently touched her shoulders and freckles that scattered around her cheeks. She collected various objects, like rocks and plants, and loved fashion. Blouses of many unique styles and colors adorned her closet from left to right. During any season, and on any occasion, she wore a blouse. That was the only thing she hated about her new job—having to stick to a standard uniform.

Kat's life was average. She was a single mom and had a stable job working as a middle-school science teacher, using her spare time to do research on the human body. She published her own works and experiments online. Up until she was thirty-four years old, everything had been completely normal. Until one day, she was laid off from her teaching job, and she had nowhere else to go. Working at another school wasn't an option at the time as no schools in the area were hiring. So instead, she had to resort to the only viable option she had—leaving the teaching profession. It was a tough pill to swallow, but she did it nonetheless.

Searching for a different job wasn't the easiest of tasks. She was only qualified in a few other areas but not enough to become a professional in anything. Then one day, a strange email piqued her interest. It was an employment request, one of high prestige and extreme rarity.

Miss Jones,

I am a representative of MLD, an up-and-coming research organization in the scientific community. I am pleased to announce that you have been invited to join our team of esteemed scientists. We offer all employees a complete 401K package, health benefits, and of course, room to grow and advance within the company. We are acquainted with your published works and based on your past record, we would like for you to start in our company as a Data Resource Tracker. Please download the attachments below for more information. Just know that this offer is an extreme honor, only given to the finest of researchers who we believe would be a perfect fit for the company (our hire rate is less than 1%). We will provide you with great working conditions and a starting salary of $90,000 per year. If you have any questions, please email me back. Thank you and congratulations!

-Margret Heisenberg

Katherine was hit with a wave of shock upon receiving the message. MLD was infamous for its secrecy and confidentiality, yet everybody knew it as the institution where only the highest-ranking scientists and researchers worked. And for some reason, they'd chosen *her*. She'd met countless people who studied their entire lives just to be offered a spot on their team. People who spent money, wasted time, simply to have a slim chance of getting employed, and at the end of the day, they were all turned down. Even getting accepted for an interview was a huge accomplishment in their eyes but not Kat. Kat was picked—exclusively wanted as a Data Resource Tracker.

Without a second thought, she instantly responded to the email, feverously typing out questions such as "When can I start?" and "What's the address of the building?" She was in high spirits, floating on cloud nine. It was the greatest honor she could've ever received.

She started her first day on the job not even a week later. She had hoped that her seven-year-old daughter Elliana would one day be proud of her and all her efforts. The only downside to it all was the uniform. Kat had to ditch the blouses and, instead, was forced to wear a blue jumpsuit. It was a small price to pay for such a special opportunity.

The building of the company was in a middle-of-nowhere town where all traffic ceased, and the busy noises of everyday life disappeared. However, amidst the barren wasteland of cornfields, stood her new place of employment—a giant office structure reflecting gorgeous shades of blues and sapphires. It was seven stories tall with tinted glass windows hiding what was on the inside and large block letters that read "MLD - Common Building." Kat was awestruck by the intricate architecture and futuristic ambience and instantly became obsessed with the institute's finer details.

The inside was no less grand than the exterior. Aromas of fresh coffee and floral soaps wafted throughout the air, as neatly organized office desks and cubicles were stationed in uniform order. As soon as she stepped foot in the entrance, a worker in a classy business suit approached her with a smile.

"Hello, there! I'm Theresa Eddison. You must be our newest addition, Katherine Jones, right?" she asked.

"Yes, that's correct. I'm very honored to be given this opportunity."

"As you should be! Here, follow me. Some of our managers will assist you during your first day of training," she began, walking alongside Kat. "Don't worry. It's not difficult at all. And besides, you're a part of our family now, which means you'll finally get to learn about some of the company secrets!"

Theresa brought Katherine into an elevator and took her all the way up to the sixth floor. However, upon stepping outside, she noticed something was very off. Instead of average run-of-the-mill cubicles and office desks, workers sat in technological chairs...

Completely unconscious.

They didn't appear to be sleeping. It was a coma-like state unconsciousness.

"Ah, what a marvelous sight! Katherine, this is what it means to be a part of MLD, aka Mid-Life Death Corporation. The heart of this operation, the very reason we are all here right now, is to study the in-between. Tell me, do you know anything about the afterlife?"

Kat hesitated, thinking of an appropriate answer. "Well, I've heard of the theories. But I don't know anything for sure," she responded. "I don't know how anyone could."

"Exactly! Absolutely nothing can be proven. Which is why the Mid-Life Death Corporation has been working to uncover as many answers as possible." Theresa raved with every sentence, every thought. "Now, answer this. What do you think happens when you go into a coma?"

"I… I'm not sure," she stammered. The slew of unexpected questions puzzled Katherine.

"Well, what if I told you that *we* knew?" Theresa started. "Here, follow me. There's something very important I want to show you."

The two walked past unconscious workers and twisted through numerous walls and podiums. Finally, they came upon the entrance of a large office. It contained holographic screens and projections of every kind, presenting images of notes and data, charts and sloppy sketches, and numbers and bar graphs. But the most important part were the lines upon lines of scripted code. There had to have been thousands of statements, stretching for miles across the perimeter. Kat was amazed at the state-of-the-art technology.

"This room summarizes the plans for the entire company. Future goals, past mistakes and experiences, everything that makes a good business successful. It also houses all the company secrets and contains classified documents which no one outside the company is aware of.

"As you already know, it is impossible to reach the afterlife and come back alive. However, we at this institution have discovered loopholes—ways around that predicament. Take a coma, for example. When a person is in a coma, they are not dead but in a prolonged state of deep unconsciousness. Therefore, they have not yet crossed over to the other side. This is what we call a usable subject. You see, it was proven a few decades ago that when a person is usable, or in a comatose state, their bodies are stationed on Earth, but the aware, conscious mind travels someplace else … the in-between, a buffer connecting the living and unliving worlds. And that, my dear, is exactly what we study." Theresa gestured outside the room, pointing at the machines and unconscious workers. "See them? All those people are currently between life and death. All it is, is a simple procedure which we perform to purposefully put you in a coma. And you, being a Data Resource Tracker, will have to occasionally 'travel' there to study information."

"Well, it definitely sounds … different," stammered Kat. She was shocked about the whole situation. One minute, she was a science teacher, telling a group of eighth graders about biohazards. The next, an experienced researcher. And while she was honored, she still couldn't comprehend why they had chosen *her*. "Don't get me wrong. It seems like very important and interesting work, but what exactly is it for? Like, what's the reason for going unconscious?"

"That's the next thing I was about to tell you. See, MLD works on behalf of a secretive organization called the Immortality Pact. It was created by the founder of this company and used for advancing immortality research. And that, my dear, is exactly what we study—*ever-lasting life*. We strive for the idea that one day in the future, every living person on Earth will be unable to die. It's the next revolutionary step for all mankind, you see." Theresa smiled with pride, swooning over the technology in the room. "Sure, we have to make sacrifices, but what's a few thousand test subjects to a never-ending bloodline of generations?"

After a few days on the job, Katherine had the training down to perfection. She quickly knew how to control a regulated coma, secretly store data files, and keep order and peace within the institution. However, she still hadn't taken a trip to the in-between. The whole idea made her sick to her stomach. Meanwhile, many of her friends and relatives had begged her to reveal MLD's corporate secrets, which she dismissed and denied, but no one really believed her. Kat knew all too well that MLD's non-disclosure policies would have dire consequences if ever broken.

Over the next several months, Katherine quickly climbed the ranks in MLD despite never going into a coma. Instead, she formed friendships and bonds with fellow colleagues. Her boss was a tenacious young woman, Scarlet Adams. She was a kind and diligent worker but gave off malicious vibes at times. It was a bit frightening when her acrylic nails ferociously tapped along solid surfaces, but overall, she was a cool person to be around. However, as Kat drew near her eighth month on the job, Scarlet became furious, impatient.

"Jones, I'd like to have a private chat with you in my office," she demanded one morning.

Of course, Kat obeyed and followed the woman into a dimly lit room. Paintings and portraits of mythology and witches hung on Scarlet's office walls, perfectly matching her personality.

"Jones, I'm sure that you're aware of this, but you've been working here for almost eight months now, and I haven't received a single speck of information from you that was recorded in the in-between. Care to explain why?" Her voice was serious and intimidating.

"I'm sorry, ma'am. I was never given an opportunity to and…" Kat began, but Scarlet didn't want to hear it.

"Miss Jones, we here at MLD have given you many opportunities. Something tells me that you just don't trust the whole 'coma' process. Which doesn't make sense, as you've performed it on others many times. Look at Theresa! She always comes back in one piece."

"I know, I'm very sorry. Please, give me a date, any date, and I'll comply."

"Unfortunately, Katherine, it is much more complicated than that. You see, the in-between has an intense energy that is very different from that of Earth's. Certain risks are involved upon travelling, and there are different regulations. You are required to take a training course on expectations and worker morality, as well as what to expect in certain situations. And, you will have to live at our Headquarters for twenty days within this ... place. In fact, I don't think you know anything at all about what you're getting yourself into. You're going to have to schedule a week's worth of guidance before your first trip, preferably with Margret when she's available. Today is a no-go as she must host an induction, but maybe tomorrow."

Kat drew a blank. Headquarters? Induction? None of it made sense.

"I'm sorry, an induction? For whom? And I thought these were your Headquarters?" she asked.

Scarlet drew in a sharp breath. "Oh dear... you know less than I thought. Get comfortable. This is going to take a while."

That night, Kat went home with an entirely new perspective about MLD. Her talk with Scarlet lasted over an hour. It was a long and arduous discussion about the truth of the in-between—what it really was, where the people really went, but more importantly, what they did. And finally, at last, she was prepared to dive into a simulated coma.

The following day, it was time for Katherine to be trained by Margret so she could finally travel to the esteemed facility.

Dr. Heisenberg's office was vastly different from the rest of the rooms. Pastel pink walls added a pop of color amid the boring whites and blues while cute decorations and tchotchkes adorned her table.

"Hello, you must be Miss Jones. It's a pleasure to meet you. I've heard great things about your work. But then again, I did choose you to partner with us. Anyway, I'm Margret, Margret Heisenberg, co-owner of this whole operation and coordinator of the facility. I believe you're here to get trained for your first time 'out there.' How exciting! It's always scary being a newbie, but you're going to be just fine! Here, take a seat," she motioned. Her personality was that of a sparkly glitter ball.

The training was simple but very detailed. Margret discussed what to expect upon arrival as well as what to do in certain situations. "When your conscious mind first enters the facility, you will wake up in a white room surrounded by security. Do not be afraid as these people will help guide you to your office and get you situated throughout your stay. You will be required to go for a twenty-day study as a Survey Analyzer, which means that you'll get assigned a new child every few hours and ask them mandatory questions while reporting their responses. These subjects will be shocked and confused, but you must keep your patience and composure. If someone acts out, hit them with a tranquilizer dart as their first warning," she said. "Though small, MLD's proprietary tranquilizer darts contain a very powerful element, *Memorant*. When injected, it causes people to experience memory loss. In smaller doses, such as the dart, the previous four minutes of the test subject's life will be completely washed and erased from their mind. For example, upon first being hit, a person will pass out for around five minutes, and then eventually wake up with no recollection of what they were originally doing. Although, when given in larger doses, *Memorant* could make a subject forget weeks' worth of events."

Margret also explained the escape rule, the way to wake up from the coma and leave the facility. "There are five mechanical chairs in the facility in total, but the one you will need to worry about is in sector Z9. After your twenty days are over, you'll get placed within the machine and use the tools necessary to help perform the trip back. It's very simple. All you must do is place the metal cap over your head and push the button on the remote. This will instantly wake you."

The final portion of the training explained how her accrued time at the facility worked. "As you already know, after forty days, the human body will be transferred from the in-between to the afterlife or, in other words, dying, as a result of staying in the facility for too long. But if one were to get out of the facility and back to the real world, their time would simply be paused. For example, if you left for fifteen days, came back to Earth, and then immediately returned, you would still have amassed those fifteen days. However, staying on Earth can take that time off. If you went to the facility for fifteen days, came back for exactly two days, and then returned, your time would sit at thirteen days because of your previous arrival. Also, switching back and forth from different worlds too frequently can cause permanent damage to your body and mind on Earth, so please, travel in your regularly scheduled intervals."

"Alright, I understand," Kat responded.

Margret slid over a sheet of paper in a manila folder and handed Kat a pen. "Great! Now, if you could please sign here? This is just a confirmation and waiver letter regarding your personal health, our confidentiality, and whatnot. According to my schedule, we can start your coma process approximately four days from today, so you better start prepping!"

She obeyed and signed the paper, filling out boxes with a sloppy signature. Now, written in black ink, was her confirmation of reaching new goals, the next step in her scientific career. She couldn't have been more honored.

When the day had arrived, she was jittery all morning, fumbling with her cup of coffee and fidgeting with her rings. She had told Elliana that she was leaving for a twenty-day work trip, and Elliana would stay with her aunt and uncle while Kat was away. Still, guilt prodded at the back of her mind.

As Kat drove up to the MLD office building, she felt as if she could no longer control her nerves. An explosion of anxiety was to burst any second, and she felt as if it would blow her up on the spot. Luckily, no such thing occurred, and she found herself walking along the pavement, nearing the front door and bravely stepping inside. Today, the air had felt different—crisper. Taking a deep breath easily relieved her of all negative emotions.

As soon as she approached the front desk, Theresa stopped what she was doing so she could assist her.

"Hey, Kat! Big day today. How do you feel?" she asked.

"Anxious, excited… everything."

"Yeah, I get that. You're going to be great. Here, right this way!"

The two walked to the central elevator, rode up to the sixth floor, and stepped outside into the abyss of unconscious workers. Except now, a chair was empty, standing tall like a grand throne—and it was all for her. Theresa guided Kat to the machine, and she gently sat atop its plush covering. Then, as if on cue, a man wearing a black suit rounded the corner, making his way over them.

"Hello! Katherine, right?" he asked.

"Yes, that's me," she responded.

"Well, hello there! I'm Steven. I'll be helping you with the coma process. Don't worry. It's quick and easy. You won't even feel a thing!" he said.

Very cautiously, he grabbed a kit of tools and pocket-sized gadgets, strapping Kat into the chair with a secure seatbelt. Then he connected a wire to the side of the recliner, each end containing a small disc-like suction cup and attached the discs to the top of her forehead. The last finishing touch—a metal cap which fit snuggly around her skull which would be the way the chip would be delivered into her brain. Meanwhile, in Steven's left hand was a remote control the size of his palm.

"Okay, on the count of three, I'm going to push the button on here, and you're going to pass out. Ready?"

"Ready," replied Kat confidently.

"One, two..."

"Three."

The transition was instantaneous. Kat didn't even feel the shift between the real world to the in-between. When she opened her eyes, Steven was no longer before her. Instead, she was in an empty white room surrounded by mysterious people in blue jumpsuits who stood in different corners. The air somehow felt different—it was an indescribable sensation. Distant sounds of light chatter came through the walls as soft muffles, and a repetitive beeping noise made her blood run cold. Despite her initial feeling of general uneasiness, Kat was quickly welcomed with open arms by the friendly staff of the facility. They gave her a tour of Headquarters and invited her to her own personal room and office in sector P8. Everyone seemed kind and accepting, and she soon fit right in with the established team of researchers.

The days were all much of the same. Every hour, she was assigned a new child subject, a newly welcomed patient under eighteen, and asked them a series of questions about their personal life. Some were confused while others were downright defiant, but the majority obeyed, simply following along with the surveys. After every response, Kat was required to store their answers and send them into a subject database while also listing any unusual behaviors they may have exhibited or acted upon. It was a simple job, and she was able to form relationships with a few of the kids. Overall, the twenty-day visit was an enjoyable experience, and she left feeling satisfied and proud of her accomplishments.

Just as Margret had promised, there was an escape chair in sector Z9. After Hours on her last night, Kat ventured there alone and set herself up within the machine, connecting the proper wires and placing the cap over her head. With the push of a button, the transition was complete, and she was awake from her coma.

Arriving back on Earth was a weird feeling. Upon regaining consciousness, Katherine opened her eyes to a dark office building, strapped onto a mechanical chair. The buzzing of scientists brought her back to reality, allowing her to take everything all in. As soon as she woke up, loud alarms sounded from the machine on which she sat, paired with a flashing green light. A worker soon approached the area with a congratulatory smile.

"Welcome back, Jones! You did great!" she cheered. "Allow me to take off those wires for you."

The kind woman helped Katherine by removing the technological gear and unstrapping her from the harness on the chair. *Back home at last*, she thought. Yet somehow, she couldn't wait for her next shift at the facility.

Years later, Kat continued her work at MLD, going to the in-between and performing many different functions and experiments. Although as time went on, things began to change, and she started to observe her surroundings from a whole new perspective. Instead of being in a hospitable environment with warm welcomes and friendly arms, the fire at the heart of the business began to extinguish, turning the previously happy atmosphere into one of doom and dread.

Workers gave her nasty looks and the conditions in the MLD office building slowly started to deteriorate. Cracks formed on walls, rust and mold grew in unusual places, and everything was cluttered and chaotic. This made people very unhappy. Katherine soon realized the twisted truth—the behind the scenes of the corporation. Kids were tortured and tested in lab rooms and chambers and were locked up within basement cells. Innocent human beings were drugged in large doses, forced to forget their past lives and conform to their new ones.

But more importantly, the higher ups recruited subjects against their will in the form of ambushes. Margret had described it as "meeting quota." Every quarter, the workers would target a specific area and unleash a catastrophic event, like a fire or an explosion. Then, during the aftermath, they'd drive up in fake ambulances and scoop up as many unconscious kids as they could. It was a corrupted system of manipulation and lies, and Kat was fed up. And so, after ten years of working as a Data Resource Tracker, she decided the truth needed to come out.

Using an alias, Kat posted on an online message board revealing many of the secrets going on at MLD. Of course, it was written as a conspiracy theory, strictly conjecture, but her thread was gaining traction on the dark web. So much traction that it was eventually brought to the attention of Dr. Scarlet Adams.

It was the morning of May 5, 2022. As she stepped into the wretched MLD building, she was immediately escorted to Adams's office.

"What's all this about?" Kat demanded when the escorts shoved her into the chair in front of Adams's desk.

"Hey, slow down there, Jones. I'm afraid we have a slight problem," Scarlet said.

"Oh?"

"My sources have confirmed that you've been quite the busy bee online. And while you're posts have been anonymous, our tech department has been able to trace the source back to you." She *tsked* her tongue on the roof of her mouth. "This is a severe breach of contract, Jones. One that is punishable…"

"I don't know what you're talking about," Kat interrupted. "You can't prove anything."

"Oh, quite the contrary. We can. And we will."

Kat nervously fidgeted in the chair. She was at a loss for words.

"Unfortunately, there's nothing else I can do except call *the boss*."

The escorts closed in on her, and Kat whipped her head around. "Wait. What?"

Suddenly, the room turned deathly silent. No busy cars driving by or birds chirping outside. It was as if the world stopped. Talking about the boss was forbidden. He was the brains, the manipulative mastermind behind all of this. The only other person who had ever come face to face with him was Margret, his number two, his personal assistant. Half of the workers even questioned his mere existence.

Scarlet jabbed a few numbers into her phone, put it up to her ear, and rested it against the crook of her neck. Finally, it stopped ringing, signaling that he, *the boss*, had picked up.

"Hello? Yes, I know, I know. We have Miss Jones in custody now. Ten years. Yeah, what do I do? Okay. Okay, got it. Thanks." The call was short, but it got the point across.

Scarlet's subtle glare made Kat uneasy. She licked her lips a few times and smiled, staring directly into Kat's soul.

The escorts forced Kat to stand, forced her hands behind her back.

"Well, Katherine, you were aware from day one that we are a highly confidential organization. You've broken that confidence. There are consequences at hand—not just for you… for your entire family."

"What do you mean? What are you talking about?" Kat sputtered, the words barely able to croak out from her throat.

With that, Scarlet motioned to the escorts, and before Kat realized what was happening, they placed a white cloth over her mouth, knocking her out.

When she awoke, she found herself trapped in the facility, where she would spend the final forty days of her life.

CHAPTER 5

It was nighttime at the facility. Fifty slept in her bunk undisturbed as Fifty-Seven's words replayed in my head like a song on loop: "I think we die." Now here I sat, watching the clock carefully as it counted down to my demise. At 11:00 pm sharp, I would make what would possibly be the biggest mistake of my life. Still, I wondered how I managed to agree to such a risky scheme…

Fifty-Seven had revealed the truth. I can't explain it, but something deep inside me just knew she was right. Maybe something subconscious in me hadn't wanted to acknowledge it, but when she said it out loud, it rang true—four dreadful words I had hoped not to hear. "I think we die."

The end-of-breakfast bell rang, signaling the start of our first class. If I hadn't just been informed of my impeding demise, I would've tried to make some friendly conversation.

"So… uh… where are you off to?" I nervously asked.

"Geometry. You?"

"Yeah, Geometry for me as well."

I hastily threw away the remains of my breakfast and placed the metal trays in the dirty tray slot. Fifty-Seven uncomfortably walked alongside me on our way to class. We were both too shocked and nervous to say anything.

The Geometry room was in sector C3. Students happily entered with their newfound friends, chatting and laughing without a care in the world.

Before we stepped inside, I turned to Fifty-Seven. "Do you really believe what you said before?" I asked, hoping for a different answer but knowing there wouldn't be one.

"Yes… yes I do."

I sighed and lowered my head. Passing Time was dwindling down by the second, and we couldn't afford to be late on our first day. With one final glance, we opened the door to the classroom and begrudgingly stepped inside.

The Geometry room was large. Rows of circular desks ran up and down the perimeter while a large whiteboard took up the length of the entire far wall. The teacher's desk was stationed in the front of the class and had various 3D holograms of different geometrical shapes. Suddenly, as if on cue, the instructor appeared from the back of the room. His hair was parted in an old-fashioned style and the strong smell of cologne wafted from his work attire.

"Good morning, students! Welcome to your first day of Geometry. I am Mr. Rinston, please take a seat anywhere," he spoke, his loud, enthusiastic voice echoing throughout.

Fifty-Seven and I hastily skipped to the nearest two empty seats as the classroom became packed with students.

"Now, let me introduce you to the power of geometry," he continued.

Just clichéd teacher jargon.

He walked over to his desk and pointed to the various holograms. "Can anybody tell me what this shape is?"

A girl in the front raised her hand. "That's a cube."

"Yes, a cube! Or so most of you may think. The energy in this facility is different than most. Watch what happens when I push one of the faces of this cube."

Mr. Rinston placed his left hand against the back side of the hologram and pushed it slightly, gradually turning it into a 2D square. A bunch of *oohs* and *aahs* erupted from the crowd.

"As you can see, the cube is now a square. But watch what happens when I do it again."

Just like before, he placed his left hand against one side of the shape and pushed, this time creating a singular straight line.

"Now, we have a line!" He stepped back and extended his arms to acknowledge the other shapes on the desk. "All of these objects were created with a very special material. It is something that was invented by the founder of this facility, called *ElastaGlass*—a stretchy and maneuverable substance that's easy to manipulate. Its purpose is to allow its user to mold different structures, and it was originally used in the architectural work around the building."

Mr. Rinston paused. "For our first unit, we will be using *ElastaGlass* to change the form of geometrical shapes while measuring their different dimensions. That being said, your first assignment will be to play around with this material and jot down your measurements and observations with the person next to you. Everyone will be given a random 3D shape, so I want you to be creative with your experimentations!"

He carefully grabbed a box of shapes and began distributing them to the class. When he came to our table, he handed Fifty-Seven and me an *ElastaGlass* sphere. It was a crystalline blue color and slightly transparent, glowing on the surface. It didn't look like an ordinary solid, but instead, had many properties of a liquid material.

I brought my finger to the rounded object and pressed the surface. The reaction was different than that of the cube, whereas the covering of the sphere went concave and formed a small dent. I wrote my observations down on the clipboard in front of me and turned to Fifty-Seven.

"What should we do?"

My question was hushed and vague, but she knew exactly what I meant. I wasn't talking about the assignment, but the fact that sooner or later, we would have to come to terms with the dire situation we were in.

We are going to die.

"We escape. That's what," she replied.

"Easier said than done. We don't know what these people are capable of," I said, and I remembered the boy who had a code yellow called on him for trying to escape yesterday.

"Then we come up with a plan. It needs to be done quickly, and we need to put it into motion as soon as possible." Fifty-Seven spoke fervently, not stopping to catch her breath.

I sighed and placed my pencil on the desk. This was all so confusing. It hurt not knowing entirely what this place was, yet maybe my gut feeling was right. From the moment I woke up here, I could sense something was off, that these workers were up to no good. But after the way they'd been treating us, it didn't seem so bad. It definitely didn't feel like I only had thirty-nine days left to live.

The light sound of a bell went off, signaling that the class had come to an end.

"Alright everybody, I'll see you all tomorrow!" yelled Mr. Rinston.

If only he knew.

Fifty-Seven and I parted ways as we went to our second class of the day. I had Anatomy Training in sector C1 with Miss Smith. It was pretty mundane with the majority of the lecture going over the basics of the human body. There were skeletal models in the room, along with prop organs and some disturbing animal samples. Miss Smith also demonstrated the body's unique reaction to pain while in the facility. On average, it took about two weeks to fully heal from a cut. However, when she used a sharp blade to pierce the skin on her hand, it only took a matter of seconds—the bloodied mark almost instantly closed. Other students were impressed, but I was only concerned. If it were that easy to heal an injury, what would it take to *kill us?*

Miss Smith also went over the rules of the infirmary. It was located in sector C9 and operated like an average clinic. She warned us that there was a certain illness present only in the facility due to the high concentration of electrical energy and radiation. *Asthenia Nervosa* was a disease that affected the ability to think and function. Her description of it was suspiciously vague, and her demeanor became very animated when talking about it. She explained that early symptoms were coughing, shortness of breath, and dizziness while the later symptoms were memory loss, motor skill complications, sleep walking, and confusion.

My stomach violently churned as lunchtime came closer. The second class finished at 2:00 pm sharp, and I ran out of the room and hurried to the cafeteria. I kept my eyes peeled, praying not to run into a certain someone.

"Hey, over here!" yelled a familiar voice. It was none other than Fifty-Seven. She was holding a wrapped sandwich in her right hand and a pencil and paper in the other.

"What's all this for?" I asked.

"I brought you a sandwich for the road. Now hurry up. We only have an hour."

"For the road? What are you talking about?"

"Listen," she leaned in closer and whispered, "if we want to escape, we need to know where we're going, right? I'm drawing up a map so we can have a visual representation of everything. Now, follow me." She quickly grabbed my hand, and we jogged away from the cafeteria.

We toured as much as we could in one hour, but truth be told, the place was huge, and there were many areas that were supervised or restricted. The lobby itself had 235 sectors that stretched for miles throughout the first floor, the intricate tiled ground clashing with the metal décor. Occasional defective lights flickered and buzzed from the grid ceiling, creating a subtle strobe effect, like something straight out of a horror movie. We walked by Headquarters to places I hadn't yet seen, even stretching beyond the conveyer belts. I didn't take much notice from when I was first here, but the facility had labeled areas that all connected at the check-in. Each area was on a different story of the building, the only form of transport being a dimly lit staircase. Twisty steps wrapped around the concrete wall as an ominous shadow of darkness clouded the unknown up above. Landings were stationed at each level, connecting the platforms, while metal trimmings outlined every individual tread, adding to the unsettling aura of all four different floors. HQ and the children's dorms were on floor one. The Landing was on floor two, where they kept the adult test subjects in separate quarters. The Science Lab was floor three, where they performed experiments of all sorts, and the Entryway was on the fourth floor—exactly what we were looking for. It was a large room guarded by security, and at the end of the hall were two big double doors. There was only one lock on the door, and the keys were in the hands of an armed military man in the center. That was our ticket, our way out, the light at the end of the tunnel. Just beyond that exit was our *escape*.

Fifty-Seven scribbled sloppy drawings onto her sheet of paper, occasionally writing quick notes. She drew up a simplistic picture of the facility, using layers to represent the different floors while labeling each one. She also wrote down useful facts about each floor, such as how many workers were present, what they were doing and what they looked like, and what were some potential obstacles in our path. In addition to that, we had to take into account any extra security precautions they might've implemented After Hours.

By the time lunch was over, we had a detailed picture of the facility with almost every relevant component. The only issue now was developing a sound escape plan.

"We should finish this up at dinner if we want to leave tonight," said Fifty-Seven.

"Right, I'll see you there," I responded.

Suddenly, the hourly bell rang. It was time for my third class of the day, Hypnosis Studies. I was a bit skeptical of the name, but figuring that I probably wouldn't pay much attention, I wasn't worried. Once again, I parted ways with Fifty-Seven and made my way toward sector C4. Before we left, she rolled up the map, placed it into her sweatpants pocket, and gave me a silent wave as we walked in opposite directions.

Upon entering the room to the class, my mood immediately changed. I felt hyper focused. My eyes were glued onto a screen in the back that flashed neon colors and bright text. A worker wearing a white jumpsuit grabbed hold of my shoulders and strapped me into a leather chair. I didn't even notice the rows of students lined up in the room. I was too focused on the video, which seemed to be playing in a loop. It contained cryptic messages and subtitles which read, "Trust the facility. We are here to help." The words felt like they were bleeding through my brain. I was lost in the cadence of the patterns and the colors. Everything was loud. The bass of the video created vibrations in the room which rocked my insides back and forth. It felt like I was going to explode. My brain was frying under the pressure, but I couldn't take my eyes away! I couldn't stop watching!

"Wake up now. It's time to wake up."

"Stella… wake up. It's time to wake up."

I opened my eyes to the blinding sunlight in my bedroom. A woman gently pushed me back and forth on the soft mattress.

"Hey, are you awake?" she asked. Her voice was calm and soothing.

I rolled over to face her. Dirty blonde hair framed her cheeks, blushing a pastel pink hue. She had a kind look on her face, one of warmth and love.

"Good morning, sleepyhead. Mia is in the kitchen making pancakes. You should get ready now." She kissed my forehead goodbye and slowly walked out of the room. I knew her—that woman was my mother.

I blinked, and the world around me transformed. Flashing white lights clouded my vision as everything moved in a timelapse, skipping and fast-forwarding. Until gradually, I began to wake up somewhere different. The scene transformed into a kitchen and a young girl had her back turned toward me. She was hunched over a stove, flipping pancakes. A jar of maple syrup and a small tray of blueberries were on the table.

"Get ready to have a breakfast like no other," she said.

She turned around to face me. Her eyes were a bright cerulean, a deep contrast to her platinum locks.

It was my sister, Mia Winterfield!

Mia set down a plate of pancakes and eggs on the table while handing me a glass of orange juice, but I wasn't focused on that. I was aware, conscious of my surroundings.

"Mia, I need you to help me!" I yelled suddenly.

"Huh? What are you talking about?" she asked.

There was so much to say, yet so little time. She needed to know about the facility, everything that happened, that I was still alive.

I tried opening my mouth to speak, but no words came out. It felt as if I were drowning in oxygen. My vocal cords were suppressed. I couldn't breathe. Suddenly, the cup of juice in my hand slipped and spilled over the kitchen tabletop, creating a huge mess. The orange liquid stained the side of the chair and dripped onto the floor, emitting a faint fruity scent throughout the room.

"Asshole, you got the juice everywhere! What's up with you this morning? You're acting like a maniac," Mia complained.

"I'm sorry. I was trying to warn you…" I began.

"Get ahold of yourself," she cut me off. "It's too early. You need to wake up."

"You need to wake up. Everybody, wake up now." I opened my eyes. I was back in the ominous classroom at the awful facility, and I was still strapped into a leather chair. I had another vision. But now, I felt different, like I had a purpose.

"There, now all of you are back with me. Welcome to Hypnosis Studies! What you just experienced was a hypnotic episode, which is what this class is all about. I am here to train and inform you all of the effects of brainwashing on the body," the teacher said at the front of the room.

Mr. Garcia continued rambling on about this and that, but I paid no mind to the lesson. The vision, or rather daydream, was the only thing I cared to think about as vague memories of Mia and my mother took shape in my mind. I wondered what they were currently doing, if they even cared that I was gone. By now, search parties and police officers had to be investigating the area, looking for any trace of where I was. *Right?* Any moment now, someone would burst through those double doors and break all of us out of here. But then again, I didn't even know what state I was in, if I was even in a state. Nobody would know where to begin looking.

Computing was my last class of the day. It was something about coding and programming on different devices, but I didn't have the heart to care. 5:00 pm drew near, meaning that it was finally time for dinner. I scanned the cafeteria tables for Fifty-Seven and eventually found her scribbling furiously on a sheet of paper.

"Hey, what's going on here?" I asked, taking a seat beside her.

"Forty-Eight, I have a plan."

My heart drummed madly in my chest. I felt sick, yet oddly celebratory at the same time.

"Here's what we do. You'll leave your dorm at eleven o'clock exactly. I'll follow five minutes later. The only thing I'll have on me will be a brick. I'll grab one from the utility closet. There's a hidden compartment next to sector M9... meet me there. Then, I'll book it for the Entryway on the fourth floor. You'll follow and chase after, as if you were trying to catch me. That way, if we get caught, you can say that you heard some commotion outside and were trying to report me to the staff. Make sure you don't wear shoes, only socks. They don't make any noise at all on these tiles. Once we get to the Entryway unnoticed, you distract the guard and

I'll use the brick to bash his head in. The one with the keys. Because although injuries heal quickly here, that doesn't mean you can't get knocked out. We'll grab the keys and break for the exit. Plan?"

It sounded risky, but it was all we had.

"Plan."

I sat in my dorm, watching the clock carefully as it counted down to my demise. At 11:00 pm sharp, I would make what would possibly be the biggest mistake of my life.

This is going to be one hell of a risky scheme.

CHAPTER 6

It was 10:59 pm. The seconds that passed were agonizing. Fifty tossed and turned restlessly in her sleep as the faint dripping of tap water echoed in the dorm.

Ten, eleven, twelve…

I fidgeted on the floor and focused on my labored breathing. The darkness of the room cast an ominous shadow on the door.

Thirty-three, thirty-four, thirty-five…

The silence was deafening. It felt as if the walls were inching closer, restricting the air around me.

Forty-nine, fifty, fifty-one…

It was almost time. I was shaking uncontrollably as the thought of all the possible negative outcomes of our plan affected my ability to think.

Fifty-seven, fifty-eight, fifty-nine…

Now.

The clock struck eleven, ending my torturous wait. I hastily opened the door, being cautious as to not wake Fifty, nothing on my feet but woven socks.

The escape had finally begun.

I crept out of the dorm into the chilly atmosphere of the lobby. Each sector was shrouded in a cloak of darkness. I heard the faint flickering and buzzing of computers in the distance and wondered for a split second if there were workers in the rooms of the sectors, but I remained focused and kept on going.

Left foot.

Right foot.

Sector M9—I needed to get to sector M9. It was hard to read the faint labels from the lack of light. Letters and numbers were just blurs from my perspective, and I simply had to go with my gut.

Left foot.

Right foot.

No stopping to catch my breath, just one foot in front of the other. That's all it was. I ran. And I planned to keep running for as long as it took. The cold air of the lobby made goosebumps travel down my arms and legs while my dirty blonde hair wildly bounced in curls above my back. It was the feeling of running free in a large cage. I hadn't actually escaped—not yet, but that breath of courage I took before sprinting away was definitely satisfying. The hallways appeared to shrink the longer I ran down them, like traversing a twisty tunnel. In fact, the farther away I was from my dorm, the more confidence jolted through my veins. I latched onto these feelings and used them as fuel, keeping my legs moving at a healthy pace as I let myself slide along the floors. Fifty-Seven was right; these socks didn't make a single sound.

And then something broke my concentration. I tripped on a thin wire. It had been carefully placed in a hidden corner of the lobby, somewhere not even people with perfect vision could see. I slammed onto the ground from the sudden downward momentum, and my head smacked the hard tile floors. My vision came in and out. Double images clouded my line of sight. Suddenly, a tranquilizer dart hit my arm. It had a slightly pointed edge and created a shallow cut on my skin from where it pierced me, but the blood stopped dripping within seconds as the cut instantly closed, just like the demo I saw in class.

Flashing white lights came into my view, and something happened… I began shifting, changing, *forgetting*. It was a trap, exactly what happened during my interview with Theresa. Another vision began to make its way through my mind as the scene around me transformed into that of my unknown past. It manifested before my eyes just like the others had. Everything was moving; everything was real. The world on the other side opened up and took me into its arms once again…

I stood outside a quaint home with blue plaster walls. Heavy rain drenched my body in cold water as I surveyed the front porch. It was my house, and I recognized every last detail. The cracks in the walls, the wooden bench, the slightly rusting mailbox. It all came back to me.

Knock. Knock. Knock.

Three knocks—all in rapid succession. I needed to get inside so I could see my family.

"Stella? Is that you? Where have you been?" my mother's voice called.

The door unlocked with a click and began to open with the hinges slowly creaking. My mom wore a fluffy black jacket and held a cup of hot cocoa in her hands.

"Stella, you're going to catch a cold. What are you doing out here so late?"

I didn't respond. I just needed to feel her warm embrace. "I'm sorry, Mom. I love you," I said, pulling her in for a tight hug.

She simply sighed and shook her head. "Honey, you should come inside. It's 11:06 pm."

"Right. Of course."

11:06 pm. Just moments ago, it was 10:59 pm. I had been anxiously waiting for it to be eleven, and then just like that, I forgot everything. Like another wave of amnesia hit me. Vague memories flashed through my mind with every passing second. I was walking, running, *escaping* from my dorm. I needed to get to sector M9 (*something about a secret compartment?*) and to Fifty-Seven. I needed to find Fifty-Seven.

It was all so strange. One minute I was sprinting down the hallway. But now, here I sat in my dorm, watching the clock exactly as I did before. The dripping of tap water made a sputtering sound from the bathroom as Fifty tossed and turned in her sleep. *Exactly as it did before!* I fell into a trap. That's what this was. Upon triggering that wire, a tranquilizer dart somehow gave me another vision and made me *forget*.

It was a struggle to remember what happened, and I tried to piece together the details. Down in the lobby, I had been pricked on the arm—that much I was certain of. The feeling of warm blood made me shiver as it eased down my frigid skin. But then, panic erupted within me, like the calm before the storm. My head seared with pain. Hot flashes burned throughout my body. I writhed on the floor to stop the pain. And before I knew it, I was back at my dorm, back at square one. *Am I in some kind of loop?*

Except now, I was ready. No more fidgeting with my fingers or counting the seconds on the clock. I was going to push through.

Just like my first attempt, I walked stealthily out the door and into the halls of the facility, ready to *redo* my escape. But when I stepped outside my dorm, something felt different—*changed*. Red laser beams projected in diagonal lines from wall to wall. *It was like they knew we were coming.* The vast room, now covered in traps, emitted a bright red aura. The beams twinkled as they shot out in different directions and turned the lobby into a scene from a high-action spy movie. Despite the traps, the lasers fortunately gave off enough light for me to see the names of the sectors, so I at least had that advantage.

I carefully maneuvered through each laser. *Leg up. Leg over. Step. Crouch.* My movements were slow and precise as I carefully bent my body in ways that wouldn't trip any alarms. I passed sectors E, F, G, quietly creeping in the dark through the security systems. I had to admit, the facility was much gloomier at night. The concrete walls were gray and aged, weathered with chips and cracks, and the red shine of the laser lights against them gave the lobby a sinister aura. I had a sense of foreboding as I wove through each obstacle, yet I pushed the feelings aside and continued trekking. Sector J1 came into view, meaning I was close, although I didn't know how much longer I could keep a steady balance. I felt like I could collapse at any second as the confident strides I previously had were replaced with a feeling of despair. I felt shaky, on edge. Every step, every crouch, made me shake. I anticipated the sound of a siren or a flashing signal of sorts if I were to make contact with the lasers.

Sector L9 came into sight. I was almost there. My breath hitched in my throat. Imaginary sounds and images teased me with each step I took, forming illusions in my peripheral vision. I got weaker. My stamina steadily declined.

Sector M3.

There was no stopping now. Red laser beams trailed behind me, seemingly moving at the same pace as me. *Leg up. Leg over. Step. Crouch.* I was dizzy. My balance became unsteady as I curled my body in that same cycle of leg up, leg over.

Sector M7.

I was right in the vicinity. Looking ahead, I could see M9 in the distance.

Sector M8.

Time seemed to slow down, and snippets of random memories flashed before my eyes, but I refused to allow my brain to indulge in them. The entrance to M9 was right there, and I couldn't allow myself to get distracted.

According to Fifty-Seven, somewhere around here was a secret compartment. As I searched my surroundings, I noticed that a portion of the wall contained abnormalities. It was a different hue than the standard concrete and looked like a clean slate, no cracks whatsoever, which I found odd considering this entire structure was worn down. I moved closer, still wary of the lasers, but once I was in reach of the strange section of the wall, I carefully knocked three times. Instead of the usual solid sound, the wall was completely hollow.

I nudged the piece of faux concrete, looking for any loose ends. After a couple of pushes, it came undone, revealing the opening that was on the inside.

"Wow, I thought you'd bail out on me." The voice was hoarse yet had a tinge of sarcasm. *Fifty-Seven.*

"You actually came? How did you get through the lasers so quickly?" I asked. The compartment of the secret room shrouded Fifty-Seven's face in a coat of darkness.

"Get in and I'll show you."

Skeptical, I stepped inside the narrow entrance and crawled my way into the peculiar hiding space. Fifty-Seven's brown hair was tied in a tight ponytail that lazily fell down her back. In one hand, she held a fragmented mirror shard.

"This," she said holding up the glass, "is our solution. We can't spend all of our time avoiding the lasers; it's too risky and time consuming. Which is why I brought this mirror with me. When reflected off of a glass surface, the light of a laser will bounce in the opposite direction. Since all of the individual beams inside the lobby are created by a singular point of light, all you'll have to do is find the source of these beams and use the mirror to change their paths. This will allow me to cross safely. Once I've gotten a steady lead ahead of you, you can follow shortly after and take the mirror with you, thus repeating the process. We're gonna have to be careful and work together on this, but I believe we can get it done."

It was a solid plan. Just change the lasers' directions, cross over, and repeat. "Sounds good. Once we leave Headquarters, the lasers should all be gone, right?" I asked.

"Right. Now c'mon. Let's get out of here."

I exited the compartment and entered back into the lobby—the danger-zone. Fifty-Seven followed closely behind. She tossed the mirror shard over to me, and the sharp edges left a small cut on my hand shaped like an upside-down V. But the cut quickly healed, and I sprang back into action. Fifty-Seven positioned herself in front of the first laser.

Stationed on the right wall was the first beam—a pocket of luminescence which projected the glowing, diagonal trap. I carefully approached it and gave Fifty-Seven a thumbs up. Then, being cautious not to touch the light, I took the fragmented shard of glass and positioned it on the floor, right in front of the source. Like magic, the laser bounced off the face of the mirror and changed its general course of direction. My escape partner got the go-ahead and made her way to the next beam. After counting to ten in my head, I crossed the deadly path of light and removed the mirror from the floor and went on to the next section.

We continued like this for a while. I'd place the mirror, Fifty-Seven would cross, I would wait, follow her, and repeat the process once we both reached the next laser. It was a tedious task but less risky and physically straining than trying to maneuver our way around. We eventually got into a flow of moving and positioning and, after a while, made it through each obstacle with ease. We were a good team, and it seemed like nothing could get in our way.

Finally, after a good ten minutes, we came to the final laser. The usual buzz of the conveyer belts was absent, signaling the dead of night. I placed the mirror down for what would be the last time, and Fifty-Seven made it across HQ and jogged to the staircase in the distance. Once she was out of my sight, I ran to make it through the final trap.

But I lost my balance.

Instead of rushing flawlessly across the tiled floor, my knees buckled and shook. By some terrible, unfortunate coincidence, my foot then slipped and collided with the glass, sending it flying across the room. I came crashing down with a loud thud. The laser was promptly redirected, hitting me square in the chest. I'd fallen right into their damn trap. *Or so I thought.* Because when I looked again at the ceiling above, all of the lasers were gone. There were no more red beams of light, no more luminescent traps to block our way. Just the vast void of an empty, dark lobby.

I stood up and dusted myself off. Everything went silent. Eerily silent. *Too silent.*

Were the lasers just a trick? Or possibly a red herring to slow us down?

A strange emptiness filled the room with a sense of dread. And then, I heard it…

Wiiiouuu. Wiiiouuu.

An earsplitting alarm rang throughout the desolate halls and red blinking lights illuminated the premises. I ran down the dark corridors, straight into the heart of the facility, not stopping to look behind me.

Left foot.

Right foot.

One foot in front of the other. I could only hope that Fifty-Seven was well on her way to the fourth floor at this point. So, I followed the familiar path she had mapped out for me—two left turns and I would reach the steps. My aching body did me no good as I sprinted down the path of the check-in.

Wiiiouuu. Wiiiouuu.

As I approached the entrance to the staircase, I heard clanging metal followed by frustrated grunts. I increased my pace and turned the corner.

Outside of the entrance, Fifty-Seven bashed a barricade with the brick she had gotten from the utility closet.

"What the hell is going on? Why haven't you started climbing the stairs?" I yelled, my voice barely a whisper above the deafening siren.

"Why do you think?" she shouted in between huffs. Metal cage bars blocked off the entrance, and Fifty-Seven's brick barely made a dent in the material. She used all her strength in an attempt to destroy it. The brick was chipped and cracked from the force, but the barricade remained standing, not a scratch on its metal finish.

"C'mon, dammit! We're so close, please!" she cried. Tears streamed down her face and gave her eyes a glossy film.

"It's not going to work," I said, keeping my composure.

"Yes! Yes, it will!" She was frantic. Desperate. Like an animal trying to escape its cage.

"Look… I need you to listen to me," I began. "Back over there, I tripped one of the lasers. They know that we're trying to escape, and any minute now, somebody is going to come around that corner and catch us. Who knows what these workers will do once they find us both? Breaking down that barricade is impossible. If you want to live, we need to come up with a way that will convince them to let us go. We need to be as unthreatening as possible, but if they see you doing *that*, it's not going to look good for us."

Fifty-Seven sobbed, and her blows to the barricade gradually became weaker until she dropped the brick and gave up on any form of escape. We'd been defeated.

"So, what should we say to them?" she asked, her voice slightly trembling.

"You can tell them I was sleepwalking. Pretend that you heard something outside your dorm and went to go check it out. I don't know. Just act like you found me here or something," I said.

Just as I had suspected, pounding footsteps echoed within the room. Five workers in high tech gear and jumpsuits emerged from the side of the room, stampeding over to the staircase and running toward us at full speed.

"Quick, pretend like you're passed out!" Fifty-Seven whispered. I did as she said and made my body go limp in her arms. I closed my eyelids and made them softly flutter.

"Code yellow, we found the targets," said Guard One into a walkie-talkie.

"Fifty-Seven and Forty-Eight, what is the meaning of this?" boomed Guard Two.

Fifty-Seven played dumb. "Ma'am, I'm really sorry, I can explain," she started. "I heard some commotion outside my dorm. It sounded bad, so I went to check. Forty-Eight was sleep walking! I think she was having a nightmare or something, so I chased after her. When she reached the stairs, she just passed out. We need help!"

"Let me look. Then I'll decide where we go from there," Guard Two instructed.

I felt myself being transferred from one set of arms to the next. Guard Two prodded my face, rubbed her nails against my chin, and stretched my eyelids open. Continuing with the act, I pretended to wake up from the sudden touch. *Remember, you don't know anything.*

"She's waking up. Come check for signs of infection," she called to one of the others.

Another worker, Guard Three, used a fancy tool to go up my nose and check my sinuses. "It's possible. Think she stumbled into the trap?" he asked.

Pretending to be confused wasn't so difficult anymore. In reality, I had no idea what was going on. The workers didn't seem too angry but rather concerned for my wellbeing.

"Where... where am I?" I asked, my voice tinged with fake exhaustion.

But it wasn't all fake-out because something within me changed. I felt dizzy, lightheaded. A cough made its way up my chest and out my throat, rattling the bones inside my chest. Then another and another. The guards' expressions quickly turned to concern.

"She's been exposed. Darrell, alert Fifty in Dorm Fifteen. Vanya, take Fifty-Seven back to HQ." The guard's grip on me tightened. "Forty-Eight, looks like you'll be going to the infirmary."

CHAPTER
UNKNOWN: PART 2

THERESA EDDISON

Theresa wore scrubs and appeared from one of the driver's seats as she shouted to the officers. "Excuse me, excuse me! I'm Doctor Theresa Eddison, here on behalf of the MLD Hospital. I have some extra room to take in the injured." She quickly flashed her badge at them.

"Oh yes, yes of course, please! We need as many hands as we can get," said the deputy.

"Alright, on it." *All was going to plan.*

In an instant, Theresa dashed inside the devastated shopping center and began looking for survivors—preferably teenagers and young adults. Through the thick smog, she trudged over dead bodies who were packed together like sardines.

What a shame. Their sacrifice meant nothing, she mused, only concerned with the project at hand.

Theresa's research had helped to develop a new plan of action—the Facility-forged Fusion Mine. It was a bomb attack used for targeting a heavily populated area. This would help them meet quota, for sure. After surveilling seventeen-year-old Elliana Jones for some time, they were able to get a fix on her location while she was shopping at the Haven Crest Mall when MLD detonated their newest device. Their target—the young woman whose mother betrayed their company.

In the end, she'd collected nine subjects ranging from ten to eighteen years old, but there was only one that she was there for. "Oh, poor Elliana Jones. We tried to warn your mother, but she just didn't listen. She had one chance to save you. Turns out, she never cared about you after all," she whispered to the unconscious girl.

"Hey, Dr. Eddison, thank you so much for your work today. This has truly been a travesty, but it's people like you who make the world a better place," one of the medics said as Theresa loaded the ambulances.

"Yes, well, I'm just fulfilling my destiny."

And with that, she hopped back into the driver seat and sped away from the scene. "Nine! I got nine patients! The boss is going to be happy with me today. Just wait until he sees my magnificent collection!"

Upon arriving at the MLD office building, all the other workers anxiously waited at their desks. They murmured and gossiped their speculations:

What will the count be?

Will it be enough to meet quota?

Will the new plan work?

When Theresa waltzed through the front door, everyone collectively held their breath.

"I have an announcement!" she sang. "Our count today is approximately... drumroll please... nine subjects!"

Gasps erupted from the office, along with subtle murmurs and whispers of "No way" or "How did she?"

"But that's not the best part," began Theresa. "I also have Jones with me! That backstabbing bastard finally got the revenge she deserved."

The eager crowd cheered in celebration and dramatically threw piles of paper into the air. It was a great day for MLD. Not only did their operation work, and not only did they meet quota, but a traitor was put right in her place. And thus, the rest of the day was crazy and chaotic as the workers threw an end of quarter party.

After the festivities, all the nine subjects were placed into MLD's test subject chairs in order to get set up in the facility. One by one, as each of the wires connected to their foreheads, every person slowly regained consciousness, drifting away to the world of the in-between.

The patients woke up in a white room surrounded by security. It was like a meeting place—the central spot where all workers and kids alike appeared. Doctors were on the scene and immediately tended to the subjects as they arrived. Without giving them a moment to breathe, or even a second to process anything, employees covered their mouths with a white cloth and sent them into a drug-induced slumber.

A few hours after their memories got wiped, the subjects were placed onto the conveyer belts where they eventually woke up with no recollection of their past lives. However, it was just the beginning of a much larger process. After their induction in the auditorium, certain kids were assigned a guide or a worker who gave them a general questions survey. Theresa was called upon at the last minute to help in the facility as a Survey Analyzer, where she was then handed a patient and required to ask them random questions. It was called the Wellness Survey, which was ironic, considering it did just the opposite. The questions had no general meaning and were only asked to see if the subjects still had any remembrance of their past lives.

As much as she wanted to question Elliana, Theresa was assigned to Stella Winterfield, renamed as Forty-Eight. The survey was off to a rough start as Stella didn't want to comply with the rules, but something within her changed midway. At first, Stella had answered with grunts and sighs, and then something like a switch went off in her head. She seemed to space out for a moment, but upon returning to reality, her perspective switched.

Or at least that's what she thought.

Right when she let her guard down, Stella pounced on the desk and snatched the tablet straight out of Theresa's hands. The world moved in slow motion as Stella violently smashed the device on the ground and stomped the screen with her feet.

Theresa was quick to act, but it was too late—the damage was already done. Nonetheless, she grabbed Stella by the shoulders and pinned her down on the table, locking her in a tight grip.

"Answer the questions next time." And then, she pulled out her tranquilizer gun and shot the girl directly in the arm.

Stella passed out instantly, leaving Theresa to clean up the mess. However, the loud commotion had gotten the attention of other workers outside the room.

"Eddison, what the hell is going on in there?" a woman yelled.

"We have a situation. I need assistance," she mumbled.

The doctor barged into the office, only to be met with a distraught Theresa, a disheveled Stella, and a broken tablet.

"Oh my word, what the hell happened?" she yelled.

"Forty-Eight lashed out, and I had to use my gun. We still have about three minutes left until she wakes up. What should I do?"

The woman paused and held a long stare. "Well, you pretend it never happened, that's what. The darts are just a behavioral precaution, so I say you grab a new device and sit right back down in that chair. Nothing worth losing your job over."

And that's exactly what she did. She pretended like it never happened. Forty-Eight woke up, visible confusion was written over her face, because there was Dr. Eddison, tablet in hand, smile on her face. Theresa knew she remembered, but it was just like that doctor had said, "Nothing worth losing your job over."

"Question two: what is your favorite breakfast food?" she inquired.

"It's pancakes. I thought you knew?" asked a disoriented Stella.

"Well, how would I know if you weren't here to tell me?"
Just control, manipulate, lie, pretend.

Just barely a day later, Forty-Eight was in trouble yet again. It was 11:00 pm, After Hours, when the workers of the MLD heard a noise in the lobby. As Theresa checked it out, she noticed none other than Stella Winterfield passed out on the floor. She'd fallen into one of their traps and, as a result, was hit with a tranquilizer dart.

"Excuse me, security. We're going to need a dorm location on patient Forty-Eight. She's been roaming After Hours," Theresa said into a walkie-talkie.

"Dormitory fifteen. Carry her back to the room. This will be her first warning," the voice on the other end responded.

"On it."

After the command, Theresa dragged Stella by her feet and dropped her off at her dorm. "Should we also activate the lasers as an extra precaution?" she asked into the walkie.

"Good idea. I'll get that set up."

The security guard turned on the lasers and continued his nightly shift, and Theresa went back to her office.

CHAPTER 7

"Forty-Eight is sick. Do you have any available rooms?"

"Only the fixups. Man, this illness seems to be spreading worse by the day. Wonder why you *others* don't seem to get sick at all though."

"Last time I checked, your assigned job was to send people in and out of the clinic and provide them with the necessary accommodations. Do not question my authority."

"I wouldn't have to question anything if your people didn't capture me and force me to do this dumb job for forty-days."

"Excuse me, but you know nothing about my people. The only person who brought you here was *you*. Now, if you don't mind, your services are of the utmost importance."

"Fine. Right this way."

36 DAYS REMAINING

When I woke up, the room was sickeningly cold. I was dizzy, and nauseous, and at a loss for words. Old machines danced in circles around me, beeping every second, mocking my helpless existence. For a moment, I thought I was back at home, expecting Mia to enter the room any second and reassure me that everything would be okay, except that fantasy never happened. I was bound to this stiff cot, rotting away in the bowels of the facility. My dreams of ever leaving this forsaken place slowly diminished with every passing second. I had failed. My throat tickled, and my stomach growled something awful. I exhaled two long, rattly coughs, and warm bile rose and slightly burned my esophagus. *Not how I wanted to start my day.*

This was nothing like the dorms. Instead of solid white walls, shades of beige and light brown stood out from all angles, cracks running up and down each surface. Lights hung from the ceiling and emitted a bright yellow hue, giving the area an unpleasant fluorescent glow. The lingering odor of death wafted in the air. From outside the closed door, I heard the light chatter and commotion of workers from the hallway. Alarms beeped with the occasional sound of a cart rustling by or the shouts of other people throughout the building. I felt sick, and my body ached all over. *This must be the infirmary.* Regardless, it sure didn't seem like a healthy living space, especially for supposedly "infected" people.

The door creaked open, and a worker wearing white scrubs entered the room. She held a clipboard in one hand and, in the other, a small container of pills.

"Hello, Forty-Eight, how do you feel?" she cooed.

I struggled to form a sentence. Words were just jumbles.

"I'm … sick?" It was more of a question than a statement.

"Yes, unfortunately. It appears that you've contracted *Asthenia Nervosa*, due to high exposure to electrical energy. Tell me, Forty-Eight, what is the last thing you remember?"

Great, so I was sick.

"Sorry… I don't … know."

"Okay, well, how about you take this medicine and get some rest? When you wake up, most of your memories should be back," she said, rattling the jar of pills in front of my face.

"Oh … kay." I didn't have the strength nor energy to argue or decline. Just take the pills, rest, and hope I woke up again.

The small tablets were blue, consistent with everything else in this facility. I cocked my head back and popped them in, washing them down with a swig of cold water. As soon as my head plopped down onto the firm pillow, I immediately passed out, entering the sea of sleep.

35 DAYS REMAINING

The start of the new day made my eyes flutter open. Tranquil sunlight filtered into the room, making it appear a bit less ominous. A plate of fresh breakfast was placed beside the bed, which I gladly accepted. I hadn't eaten in what felt like forever.

The pills had definitely done their job. My mind was cleared of all confusion, and most of my body aches were gone. But I still felt *off*—like a part of me was still sick, still damaged. Luckily, my severe symptoms had almost magically disappeared, and I seemed to get my memory back as events from the nights before played back in my head. *Who knows how long it's been since our failed escape*? As those thoughts crept into my mind, the door to my room slowly opened once more, revealing a worker in a blue jumpsuit and another figure trailing behind her.

"Good morning, Forty-Eight. If you don't mind, there's a visitor who would like to speak with you," said the woman. The girl appeared from the shadow of the nurse, revealing a familiar someone.

Fifty-Seven.

She appeared to be in better shape than me, yet she was still a bit disheveled. Bags were under her eyelids, and her face was drained of all color.

"Yeah… that's fine," I mustered. Talking was a bit easier now.

"Very well then. You have ten minutes." And with that, she stepped out of the room, closing the door behind her and leaving me and Fifty-Seven alone.

"Hey," she said in barely a whisper.

"It didn't work, did it?" I asked, hoping that maybe this was all a bad dream.

"No, we failed."

I closed my eyes and released an airy breath. It was all true. "So… what happened?"

Fifty-Seven sighed, brought a chair next to my bed, and slumped down onto the metal seat. "Well," she began, "a lot happened. That was four days ago, our attempt. Right after you directed the last laser, I began booking it to the staircase. But when I arrived… well, it was blocked off, barricaded. I tried using the brick to destroy the metal cage, but it didn't work. I couldn't even put a dent in it. A few seconds later, it went from total silence to—Boom! Alarms. Bright red lights flashed everywhere., and I couldn't hear a thing.

So, I just kept trying to break into the staircase. There was nowhere else to go, nothing else to do. You showed up not shortly after, screaming some inaudible nonsense. I don't remember what you said, but I had given up on escaping at that point. My brick was all tattered and chipped. Until you came up with a last-minute idea that saved both our asses, man! I mean it. The workers and guards appeared out of nowhere, but you just crashed into my arms, pretending to be asleep.

I followed your story—said you were sleepwalking and ended up passing out there. But then something unusual happened. The guards looked awfully concerned, and I couldn't tell why. One of the guards scooped you up, and some other guy inspected your face. Kudos to you for keeping up the act because I would've completely blown it all up at that point. I was about to burst out laughing because what a scene it was! Until you began coughing. And not just a tickle-in-my-throat cough but a full-on bone-rattling, chest-wrenching cough. And then the guard that was holding you said you had been exposed. The rest from there was pretty much a blur. Some worker grabbed me by the arm and dragged me along the floor of the lobby. I thought we were busted until she brought me to her office and started asking me a slew of questions: 'How long was she asleep for? Did she have any symptoms previously?' And x, y, z. I just had to play along. I made up a whole separate story just piggybacking off of our own. The lie was pretty unbelievable, but it got the job done. And then, they just let me go back to my dorm, back to reality. Look… what I'm saying is, we didn't escape, and yes, you did get sick, but that might have just saved us both. Nobody suspects a thing, and we're still alive! I mean, how 'unlucky lucky' is that?"

I stifled a laugh and turned to look away from Fifty-Seven. "I'm sorry. You know, for botching our escape plan."

"Hey, don't apologize. Regardless of whether you tripped the security system or not, there's no way we could've gotten past that barricade," she said. "Which brings me to my next point. If we ever want to leave this place, we're going to have to figure out how to deactivate that thing. It's impossible to break, but it's not down 24/7, which means that there's some sort of button or switch to turn it on or off."

I sat upright in the bed, thinking about our dire circumstances. My being sick didn't make things any better.

The door to my room opened again, signaling that it was time for Fifty-Seven to leave. I gave her a departing nod. A worker ushered her out. She came back in, took my empty breakfast dish, and sat down on the edge of my bed to talk.

"So, Forty-Eight, how do you feel now? Any better?"

"Yeah, I'm doing okay. Do you know when I'll get to go back to my dorm?" I questioned.

"Well, sweetie, if you want to do that, we need to make sure you're fully healed. So, it is mandatory that you take a quick set of tests before you leave."

Perfect. Mandatory testing. Just what I need.

I cocked my head and looked at her. "And when will I have to take these tests?"

"Whenever you'd like, but if you fail, we will be forced to keep you here for another few days. It's our policy," she warned.

"In that case, I'd like to take them today," I said, feeling a rush of confidence.

"Are you sure? Like I said, if you fail, it's necessary that you stay here longer."

"Yep, sure."

"Alright then!"

The worker walked up to a phone at the end of the room and dialed the front desk. The voice on the other line was inaudible to me, but by the look on her face, she didn't seem too pleased with what was being told to her. The conversation ended with a few subtle groans before the woman plastered on a fake smile.

"Well, there's a bit of an issue. All of our testing chambers today are fully booked, and we can only get you in After Hours. Would that be okay?" she asked.

After Hours, not After Hours. What did time matter to me?

"Sure, that's fine," I said.

"Great! Just to go over the basics, the test will involve strategical and physical challenges. Since *Asthenia Nervosa* can affect the ability to move, think, and function, you will be asked to perform specific tasks with full accuracy."

"Got it." It was 1:00 pm, meaning that a class was in session. Just a few more hours until I could take the test and be done with this place.

The worker left the room with a lighthearted smile, leaving me on my own. All of this was so confusing. One minute I was performing a high-action escape, the next, bed bound in a clinic. I wasted days just rotting on this firm mattress, living off dreamless sleep. Yet in the midst of this entire operation, I still didn't know why I was here. I had a mother who loved me, a sister who cared for me, a new friend, maybe even dreams and goals for the future.

But they were all gone at the hands of these people. *And for what?* I wondered how many others they destroyed and killed, ripped away from their lives and brought to a facility where they were told to listen and obey. How many people would've grown up to be actors, inventors, teachers, or surgeons? How many already *were* those things? Kids studying to get their degrees, adults desperately trying to fix their broken pasts, young girls who were carefree, who loved going shopping and hanging out with their friends. All of our individuality, our personalities, were stripped away the moment we opened our eyes in this damn place. *Oh, but don't worry, you were brought here for a reason.*

A reason for me? Or a reason for them and their own benefit? So I can be treated like a statistic or some sick lab rat? Yet I couldn't help but laugh at the irony of it all because in the end, that's all I really was—*a sick lab rat*. It was the same reason I had to take these tests. They didn't want to see if I'd gotten better. They wanted to see how the disease affected me, like I was the variable in their complex experiment.

Later on, they'd happily giggle in their little beige cubicles and type all of the data into their blue laptops, comparing and contrasting the results of me and Sixty-Five, me and Ninety-Two, or me and Eighty-Four. We were numbers, percentages, pie charts, and bar graphs. Mere pawns in their twisted game—not people. I wasn't even allowed to tell the others my own name. My identity was gone, a figment of the past, a past which I had little to no recollection of, a past that I would never be able to get back to.

People say to make the most of the time you have left, but what is there to do in thirty-five days when you're stuck in a science laboratory? Plus, there was no contact with the outside world whatsoever. Sure, there were windows and glass panels stationed around the facility, but they never looked out anywhere. It was simply a manufactured projection of light that followed a twenty-four-hour day-night cycle. I didn't even know where I was. Was the facility somewhere underground or just a figment of my imagination? There came a point when time didn't feel real, that I was just existing in a manmade simulation of sorts, and that my life had been fractured. But those were just intrusive thoughts—nothing more, nothing less.

The minutes passed by like a slowly burning flame. Every second I spent in the bed was agonizing and dreadfully long. There wasn't much to pass the time except for a stack of books beside my cot. One of them was familiar, a big purple book with gold edges with a dragon on the cover. It was what I'd read my first morning here, the same day I tried to escape. My roommate Fifty had woken up bright and early to complete some morning chores. I remembered being so aggravated that I read to tune her out and pass the time. It was funny to think, but I missed it.

I missed my annoying roommate and her pesky cleaning habits. And now, I didn't even understand why I hated her so much. It was all due to my own pettiness, the way I perceived her when we first met. The look she gave me was full of disgust or so I thought at the time. And her constant cleaning was never-ending! Although now I understood why she did what she did. The infirmary was a mess, and I would do anything to share a room again with a hyperactive neat freak. But I guess you only miss something when it's gone.

Seconds turned into minutes. Minutes into hours. Before I knew it, it was already Common Hour, at least for the normal people—the ones who weren't sick. Fifty-Seven never came to visit again, presumably because of her classes, and Fifty didn't show at all. I was a little hurt, but how could I blame her?

The workers came in to give me dinner not too long after Common Hour began. It was similar to what I ate my first night here: a microwavable meal. This time, I had pasta with meatballs and a miniature side salad. I ate it all, despite not having much of an appetite, and continued waiting until 8:00 pm when the testing would finally begin.

When it was officially After Hours, a man wearing blue scrubs made his way into the room. He sported a nametag that read "Steven," and round glasses perfectly framed his plump face. His black curly hair was gelled back into heaps on the top of his head.

"Hello, Forty-Eight. I'm here on behalf of the MLD psychology unit, co-manager of 'The STO,' also known as 'The

Sick Testing Operation.' You requested to be evaluated at this time. Am I correct?"

"Yes, correct," I answered.

"Great! Come right this way. Shall we begin?"

CHAPTER 8

I was overcome with a wave of emotions as my feet hit the solid ground. It was like taking my first ever baby steps. Sure, it had only been four days since I last walked, but the feeling was truly freeing.

Left foot.

Right foot.

The swift motion of my legs as they went one in front of the other felt as if I were gracing a majestic, far away land—a land of magical grandeur and fantastical creatures with humans manipulating elements in the wild. But of course, those were just fantasies. I was still in the rundown, God-awful infirmary.

Maybe that's why I love fantasies so much.

As Steven brought me down the halls of the gloomy clinic, I saw things not even present in my worst nightmares—nothing at all like a fantasy. It was chaos in its purest form: clutter, disarray, death, sickness, filth, disorganization, stress. Every corner we turned, every room I investigated… pure and utter *chaos*. As we drew nearer to the Testing Chambers, the lights slowly dimmed, and the tunnels darkened in shades of blue and fuchsia, deep purples which projected a whimsical glow. The odors began to lift, and the air became clearer, making it easier to breathe.

Soon we came to a room with solid black doors. Golden locks linked around the front, revealing twisty chains and metals of all sorts. Steven reached into his pockets and pulled out a matching golden key, perfectly inserting it within the body of the lock. Then, in one swift motion, the doors opened in a dramatic fashion, revealing the splendor on the other side. Right in front of my eyes, I marveled at the glory of the vast room, the Testing Chambers.

Walls painted in pure black and blue, gadgets like none I had ever seen—it was the heart of the facility, a treasure trove of riches and magnificence, the renaissance of the older dark ages. Robots and cosmical machines, very much unlike the tacky ones in the clinic, sparkled with mirrors and flashing neon colors. Simulations, technological workings, and complex constructions were all stationed throughout, as intricate wires and futuristic implements blinked and beeped with every subtle movement. It was a beautiful haven of abstract AI, a visual representation of society's advancements. Computers shaped like living creatures gazed at me through their "eyes," cameras which shuttered and flashed, creating beams of light in my direction as if I were a prized possession, a celebrity on the world stage. Portal-like crevices illuminated the ground on which I stood, wrapped in rings of LEDs which transferred lines of code from one device to the next, like nerves making their way to the brain. I was awestruck by the architectural and historical innermost workings of the room. The Infirmary and the Testing Chambers were like night and day, as if I were visiting two completely different worlds. This place represented the world of the future, what it was like being surrounded by technology and robots who were smarter and more advanced than mankind. It surely was a sight to see.

"Forty-Eight, right this way, please! And watch your step," Steven said. As I observed my surroundings, he guided me toward a large human-shaped machine, one that I could step through. It was covered in an abundance of *ElastaGlass* which acted as a screen.

"Our first test is going to be a bone and muscle examination to make sure that nothing is physically damaged. So I am going to ask you to step through the *ElastaGlass* covering. It will feel strange at first, but you'll get used to it. Once you're fully submerged, you'll simply position your arms against the arm rests to make a 'T' shape with your body. The test will take about three minutes to fully scan and render, so brace yourself and remain as still as possible," he instructed.

I nodded and waited for the go-ahead to begin the test. Once Steven gave me the thumbs up, I physically prepared myself and made my way to the inside of the machine.

ElastaGlass. The material invented at this very facility. It looked like a projected image, a hologram, but upon handling it in Geometry class, it felt more like a jelly substance. I couldn't fathom the why or the how, but I guess that was never important. As I stepped up to the entrance of the machine, I made my way directly toward the material, just like walking through air. It was thinner than water, but thicker than gas and completely transparent, meaning I could see everything around me. The first few seconds didn't feel like anything out of the ordinary until I was fully submerged within the atoms, and my experience drastically changed. The temperature in the room dropped from lukewarm to an icy chill, freezing every fiber and bone in my body. The stretchy material solidified around my frame and created a perfect imprint of where I stood, literally caving in on itself. My muscles tensed and compressed with every passing second, and it felt like all the blood in my body would seep from my pores at any given moment.

Despite the uncomfortable atmosphere, I complied with the rules of the test and lifted my arms into place, so they gently sat atop the rests. Immediately, a green light flashed from within the machine, panning up and down my body as if to scan every last inch. Robotic voice commands sounded from the various devices outside, but the *ElastaGlass* made it so I couldn't hear a thing. Monotone mumbles and generated gibberish were the only noises I could hear.

Steven was right. After a couple of minutes, the strange sensations I felt upon first entering the structure were almost completely gone, nothing but a fleeting memory. It was oddly therapeutic, despite the circumstances, and I let the cold substance encase my body, almost like relaxing in a frosty icebox. Pretty soon, the panning green light disappeared, signaling that the test was complete. Steven called me over, and I carefully stepped through the *ElastaGlass* covering once more, exiting the machine.

"Well, Forty-Eight, looks like you've checked out on this first test! I didn't see any abnormalities or problems regarding your bones or muscles, which means that you will move on to the next course. Please, follow me, right this way," he ushered me on.

It continued like that for another two hours. Steven would perform various tests, take notes, and then lead me to the next section. Sometimes, I would be asked general knowledge questions, such as random facts about my life and what certain objects were. He'd sit me down in a chair and project images of things on the wall behind him, like a color or a shape.

"Okay, look at the picture now. Can you tell me what color this is?"

"Red."

"Very good! Anything specific about it?"

"It's dark."

"Well done! Next..."

His voice was fake and condescending, as if I were five years old.. There was just something about it I absolutely couldn't stand. Every time I correctly answered one of the simple questions, he'd clap and gesture, saying nice affirmations and words of encouragement. It made my blood boil something awful. Just another reason why I had to leave this place. That thought was what kept me going, what kept me from losing my cool. Without it, I would've flipped every table and chair I saw, cussed out every worker I met, and ripped up every beloved piece of data I could get my hands on. Papers and papers of data, vital information, and research based around our lives—I'd take every sheet and tear it up like a ferocious animal if I could. Then they'd have a real reason to lock me up.

There were also more physical tests. Some involved machines, and others required me to do something active, like stretching or balancing. Steven observed my knee strength, arm strength, and lower body strength, but most importantly, my head. Whether it was being compressed in a strange contraption or scanned from the eyes of a robot, he was always studying and probing my mind, my innermost thoughts and secrets. It was what these people wanted. They wanted to see inside each and every one of our brains to dissect us and turn us into their pet projects. I was just contributing to this mess of an experiment.

Meanwhile, Steven's black eyes somehow sparkled with fervor and madness upon conducting each test, each trial. His rounded fingers giddily flipped each page of his notebook, like a child opening presents on Christmas. I've never seen someone so engaged in their job before. Mathematical equations and other various observations filled each section of the journal with loose notes lazily written in the margins. He was a true mad scientist. If anyone was ever going to take over the world, I was confident that it would be him, no doubt about it. The crazed look in his eyes said it all.

Finally, after the plethora of exams were completed, Steven took me out of the Testing Chambers, through the Infirmary, and down the hall into a quaint office. The stench of mystery substances wafted into the air once more, making my nose scrunch in disgust. However, the office to which I was brought to was vastly different from the rest of the clinic. The simplistic beige walls were perfectly paired with tan leather chairs. Meanwhile, higher-ranking workers sat at the head of a large table, sipping on what appeared to be alcoholic beverages. The woman at the front, Margret, looked to be the boss of the other executives. She was the same lady who coordinated our induction the day I arrived at the facility. Her bouncy blonde hair and fake smile was as obnoxious as ever. A stack of papers was neatly placed in a pile in front of her, untouched and ready to be evaluated.

"Hello, Forty-Eight. Please, take a seat," she coaxed. Her presence was bold and intimidating.

I sat across from her, Steven following suit. As we got settled, she cleared her throat, breaking the tension in the air.

"As you know, not too long ago you contracted *Asthenia Nervosa*. Today, you immediately wanted to be tested, despite the risk that came with failure. Well, I am here to tell you your results."

My body tensed up. After each trial, Steven had simultaneously typed out the data and sent it to an unknown printer. At least now I knew where all the papers had been going.

"Forty-Eight. I am here to tell you that you absolutely…" She paused.

The air was suffocating. I could hardly breathe.

"Passed! Congratulations, your test was a complete success. You mastered everything from physical skills, to thinking, reasoning, and memorizing. Which means that your stay at the Infirmary is officially over. We will be sending you back to your dorm right away."

I could breathe again. Finally, I would be going back to normalcy or as normal as my life could possibly get. *At least I didn't fail!*

I didn't even realize that I was walking out of the office and down the clinic halls when a slight sound made me jump back into reality. It was the noise of an alarm, and it was coming from the woman escorting me back to my dorm. She grabbed a walkie-talkie that hung from her pants and turned it on, sending a signal to the other part of the facility.

"Calling to sector Z5. It's ten o'clock. Bring it down."

Maybe it was my sudden curiosity or the great mood I was in, but either way, I was intrigued.

"Excuse me, but what does that mean? Bring it down?" I asked.

The worker turned toward me and chuckled. "We're closing up the stairs. Every night at ten, there's a barricade we activate in order to block off the entryway to the other floors."

Sector Z5, stairs, barricade. It all made sense now. The woman continued to ramble, but I wasn't listening.

"… we don't put them down directly After Hours since a few security guards stay on watch. But their shift ends not too much later, and we need to protect this place at all costs."

"I'm sorry. You said there's a barricade you put down by the stairs. How do you activate it?" I asked, my mind racing with a slew of thoughts. *This is my ticket.*

"There's a button we have to push every day. Other workers are supposed to keep watch over it at night, but they often fall asleep during their shifts. Lousy pieces of crap they are."

A button in sector Z5 that activates and deactivates the barricade with little to no security. This was perfect, exactly what we needed to escape.

I wanted to ask more questions, but my dormitory came into view, ending my walk with the worker.

"Well, looks like this is you. Have a nice night, Forty-Eight," she kindly said. There was no fake façade, no wall of faux cheeriness, just genuine sympathy, the first I'd seen in a while.

As I stepped inside the room of the dorm, it looked exactly like how I left it. Organized furniture, color coded décor, and spotless floors made it sparkle and shine in every way possible. In the midst of it all was Fifty, sitting at a desk while furiously scribbling notes on a sheet of paper. *Fifty*, the same girl who gave me dirty looks on the conveyer belt. The same girl who hyper organized our room the first morning we got here. I should've hated her guts, yet I was glad to see that she was still in one piece.

"Welcome to hell," she remarked.

"No," I began, "I just got back. What are you doing up?"

"Work."

I sighed and made my way to my bed. The silence in the room was loud, so I decided to start some friendly conversation.

"At least you're not in the Infirmary. That place was rancid. Filled with disease and death."

"Sorry, but do you want something?" Fifty snapped, slamming her pen down on the desk.

I was taken aback by her change in demeanor. "Oh, I was just trying to make small talk," I said, disregarding her rudeness.

"Yeah, well I don't wanna talk to a *traitor*!"

My body froze. Maybe it was a twist of the tongue or a spur of the moment comment. Either way, her language struck me as odd.

"I'm sorry… a traitor? What do you mean?"

"You know damn straight what I mean! How *dare* you go against the facility's teachings? I hope you're ashamed of your behavior, you stupid asshole, 'cause karma is going to eat you *alive*," she yelled.

"What the hell is going on? Where did all of this come from?"

"You know where. The fact that you tried to *escape* is sickening and after all these people have done for you! You're a bastard, Forty-Eight, you know that?"

"After all these people have done for me… are you serious? Do you even know why we're here? Do you know why we're being treated like *animals*?" I pleaded.

"We are here to help the facility revolutionize technology by participating in experiments for the greater good. Anyone who can't see that is dense and blind."

"You're wrong, Fifty, and you goddamn know it!" I yelled, slamming my fist against the table. "They are *using* us! We're the damn pawns in this whole screwed up game! Subjects, lab rats, whatever you want to call it, it still means the same thing in the end."

"That's not true. I'm important, and without me, this entire operation would crumble to the ground. Can't you see that it's our destiny? Just imagine the scientific advancements. Don't you want to be a part of that?" Fifty asked in a sing-song voice. It was strangely hypnotic and almost lulled me into a false sense of security.

Almost.

I had it with her. Anger boiled within the pit of my stomach like hot, bubbling water. I felt it rise up and out of my throat, taking control over my body. Then suddenly, without thinking, I grabbed the front of her shirt and violently shook her back and forth. "You asshole! Open your fucking eyes! This isn't some grand fantasy or lifechanging experiment. You're not benefiting from anything, goddammit! Because once these people are done with us, we're sure as hell getting replaced!"

"Get your hands off me, bitch! What the hell are you saying?"

"What I'm saying is that after forty days in this damn facility, we're both going to die!"

The room became dead quiet. Fifty didn't move a muscle or say a single word. It was pure silence. And as I stared directly into her eyes, a subtle green flare crossed my line of sight. Embedded within her irises was the image of a computer chip. It blinked and beeped with numbers and lines—like it was programming, *manipulating*, her innermost thoughts. And then, it dawned on me...

This is what they want.

I let go of Fifty's shirt and rushed toward the bathroom, locking the door behind me. After a flick of the switch, the luminescent lights turned on, and I analyzed my face in the mirror, poking and prodding at the skin along my eyelids. Deeply embedded in my blue eyes was that same technological imprint, a green data chip which scanned and programmed my thoughts. Except mine was different—mine flickered and buzzed on and off, sending out lines of static and malfunction. *It is broken.* That's what gave me the free will to think, the reason why me and Fifty-Seven weren't completely brain-washed. We were the outliers among the herd of sheep.

"Forty-Eight, what the hell happened? Are you okay?" Fifty yelled as she relentlessly slammed on the door, trying to break through.

"Nothing, just … washing up."

"I know that's a lie. Did you see a damn ghost or what?"

"Yeah, something like that," I replied.

She stopped her assault on the door. "Whatever, I'm going to bed. Just know that you are officially on my shit list!" With that, she walked off, leaving me alone in the bathroom.

I was exhausted beyond measure. As I went to bed that night, all I could think about was my conversation with Fifty, the data chip I discovered, and my revelation with the stair-case button, which I had yet to tell Fifty-Seven about. I was still confused, still in pain, and still lost within this weird world. Yet only one question remained as I drifted off into dreamland…

Where am I?

CHAPTER 9

I watched the clock carefully as it counted down to my demise. At 11:00 pm sharp, I would make what would possibly be the best, yet worst, decision of my life. Except now, I was ready—ready for anything the world wanted to throw at me.

This was it.

34 DAYS REMAINING

The long night of arguing with my roommate was over, and soon it was morning which meant back to reality—back to *escaping*. I needed to get to Fifty-Seven and tell her about the button since it was the only way we were ever going to get out of here.

I took a quick shower, threw on my clothes, and attempted to make myself look presentable in as little time as possible. I brushed my teeth, fixed my hair, and got my supplies in order. Ten minutes before breakfast started, I ran out of the dorm and made my way toward the lobby. My eyes were peeled for the only person in this facility I could trust: Fifty-Seven.

In the midst of all the chaos and clutter in the cafeteria, she had her back up against a wall, reading a book without a care in the world. There was no sign of emotion on her freckled face, just boredom and mild relaxion. I thought if I wanted to make my plan work, we had to spend the least amount of time together as possible; otherwise, we'd look suspicious. With that in mind, I raced over to where she stood and interrupted her reading session.

"Hey, I need to make this quick. Just pretend I was never here," I whispered.

"Woah, you're back from the infirmary? You don't look sick anymore!"

"Yeah, I'm not," I stated, dismissing her concern. "Anyway, this is important. About that barricade that got in the way of our first plan, I know what to do about it. There's a deactivation button in sector Z5 with minimal security. The workers push it every night at 10 o'clock to cage up the stairs. I want you to meet me there tonight at 11. Take another brick with you. We're going to infiltrate Z5, find the button, push it, and then run like we've never run before, understand?" Since leaving the infirmary, the only thing on my mind was planning our escape. Now, knowing the location of the deactivation button to the stairs, I was finally able to put my plans into motion.

Fifty-Seven's eyes went wide with shock. "Yes, I understand. But what do we do from there?"

"Once we get to the Entryway on the fourth floor, you're going to carry me. Pretend like I've been infected and ask the head guard for some help. The same guard holds the door key—the key for the exit. He should be the only person there.

Once he gets close enough to inspect me, take your brick and bash in his head. Then, we leave. Simple as that."

"Look, it's a decent plan, but that's easier said than done," she urged.

"I know, but it's either this or nothing, right? I'm leaving at 11 o'clock. If your ass doesn't show up to sector Z5 within five minutes, I'm doing it all alone. Goodbye, Fifty-Seven."

And with that, I walked off to a separate part of the cafeteria. I was as determined as ever, whether Fifty-Seven joined me or not. The powerful feeling of confidence surged through my veins, making my heart skip a beat, because this time, I wouldn't fail. This time, I was *ready*.

It was 10:59 pm. I was just seconds away from finally leaving. Fifty was sound asleep in bed without a clue as to what I was doing. The thought of being able to see my family again was what kept me going. It's what gave me purpose.

Three, four, five.

I closed my eyes and counted.

Ten, eleven, twelve.

Time seemed to freeze.

Twenty, twenty-one, twenty-two.

Any moment now.

Forty-three, forty-four, forty-five.

I was finally going to leave.

Fifty-seven, fifty-eight, fifty-nine.

Now.

I quietly opened the door of the room and slipped away into the darkness of the lobby. There weren't any lasers this time which meant we could take them by surprise.

My feet landed in succession on the tile floor.

Left foot.

Right foot.

I couldn't see anything, but sector Z5 was one of the last rooms. All I had to do was make it to the end of the hall. The rushing wind as I sprinted through the lobby gave me force and momentum while my hair bounced wildly in curls above my back. I got into the sweet rhythm of marching around. Running and bending my legs in a constant motion felt like dancing on an open stage.

Once again, there was nothing on my feet but woven socks. The white cloth gently glided along the ground and muffled the thumping noises I created from sprinting. Waves of dizziness occasionally caught me off guard, indicating some after-effects of the illness and medications. But I pushed through. Nothing could break my stride. Nobody could get in my way. A sickness wasn't about to make me give up.

As I ran down the halls, I wondered if Mia would do the same thing for me. Would she sacrifice her life, put all or nothing on a half-baked escape plan? Whatever the answer was, I frankly didn't care. This was my decision. It was risky, but it was mine because in the end, I'd risk it all for family. No matter the cost, no matter the consequences. I would do this and so much more. I willingly and knowingly put my life on the line. Hell, I was running down an ominous facility hallway in an attempt to break out. If that wasn't proof that I would do anything, then I didn't know what was.

I wandered the lobby for what seemed like forever. Sectors upon sectors whizzed in and out of view. "K8- Communications." "N7- Kitchen." "V2- Woodworking." Rooms which held no significance seemed to pass by for ages. An occasional blink of light or subtle noise would often break the dull atmosphere of the facility. I just kept running.

I saw the wall at the end of the lobby in all its cracked and corroded glory. Sector Z5 was finally upon me. A low hum rang from the inside of the office, the familiar sound of somebody snoring. This was my perfect opportunity. Nonetheless, I decided to stay true to my word. Fifty-Seven had five minutes. Whether she came or not was completely up to her.

The seconds were agonizing as I waited outside the sector. Fatigue struck me at the speed of light, as hallucinations which manifested from the darkness played tricks on my mind, keeping me company. I was hungry, tired, lost, confused. Yet the one thing I wasn't, was *scared*. Time passed in the lightless lobby. My eyes began to droop. My confidence withered. It had been long past five minutes, yet I held out hope that she would come. And so, I waited. I waited until the hallucinations died down and the imaginary sounds in my mind began to quiet—until all that was left was me and my hope. My stupid, false, good-for-nothing hope.

Thirty minutes.

An hour.

I waited. Nobody showed. Fifty-Seven had bailed on me after all. There would be no escape. All of the previous confidence I had was gone, replaced with disheartening despair. I got up from the floor and started making my way back to the dorms. Finally, I heard it. *Footsteps. Running.*

A figure appeared from the shroud of darkness. It was a girl, the same girl with that ever-so-familiar brown hair and freckled face. Fifty-Seven. Her clothes were tattered, and her hair was in a mess of knotted curls, but it was her. As she approached, her features became much more visible, accentuating the state of disarray she was in. But none of that mattered now. My confidence returned. My hope was replenished. Escape plan 2.0 was officially in motion.

"Please, don't leave without me! I changed my mind. I didn't think the plan would work, but there's nothing else we can do. I'm sorry, Forty-Eight," she whispered.

I waved my hand in front of my face to dismiss her apology. "It's fine. You got the brick?" I asked.

"Yes ma'am."

"Alright, let's go."

And with that, we were off, venturing into the unknown of sector Z5. Our footsteps were quiet and muffled as we approached the tall steel doors. Bolts and screws of various metals were sticking out from the hinges, giving the exterior a strangely ominous vibe. Fifty-Seven grabbed ahold of the bar in front and pulled, using all of her strength to open the entrance. Steel rubbed up against the tile floor, creating a low-rung creak that scratched and chipped at the ground, a sound which was anything but discreet.

The inside was nothing out of the ordinary. Cubicles, desks, and office chairs were placed in every square inch of the room. The only noise was the faint snoring of a sleeping worker on their shift. Luckily, our entrance wasn't enough to rouse him from his sleep.

I motioned for Fifty-Seven to follow me and tiptoed my way over to the source of the sound. Small flashes from inactive computers gave us flicks of light amid the blackened space. Besides that, we were all we had when it came to navigation.

The snoring got louder as we passed by mazes of walls, signaling that we were close. Suddenly, a mop of black hair came into view, coiled in bouncy curls above the person's head. They were shrouded in darkness from a distance, and as we got closer, we saw the male worker sleeping on his shift. Sitting on the table beside him was the very object that I had been searching for—the sacred item which held the ticket to our escape, *the button*.

I approached it, marveling at its bold red glory. White block letters were etched onto its surface, labelling it, confirming that it was exactly what we needed. Just as I was about to touch the top of it, feel the weight of it under my fingers, something stopped me. A large glass covering locked it in from all angles. A keyhole rested along its sides, mocking me, torturing me with every passing second.

Fifty-Seven pointed to the button with a questioning look. I simply nodded but cringed while making key-unlocking motions with my hands. However, she didn't seem too upset over it. As if it were a natural instinct, she took the tan brick from out of her sweatpants' pockets and handed it to me.

What is this for? I spoke through my eyes and movements.

You're going to break the glass ... with the brick, she motioned.

What?! No way! I'll get caught!

Hello? That's what I'm here for. Trust me. Destroy the glass. I'll deal with the rest.

I didn't exactly think this was a good idea, but we'd already come this far. There was no backing out now. I took the brick from out of her hands and held it above my head.

Just break the covering. It's that easy.

Up. Back. Forward. Down. Smash.

Up. Back. Forward. Down. Smash.

Up.

Back.

Forward.

Down.

Smash.

The earsplitting shriek of shattering glass filled the silent room. Fragmented shards, bits and pieces of the remaining case—it all came crashing down. The black-haired worker abruptly woke up from his slumber. Disorientation and confusion were written all over his face. Meanwhile, a mad look twinkled in his eyes as he saw what I had done. In a moment's panic, he haphazardly reached for the walkie-talkie strapped at his waist. Other various items spilled from his pockets upon doing so—a deck of cards, *a tranquilizer gun.*

"Code yellow! We have a code yellow! I repeat, we have a code…" His cries were suddenly cut off. Before I could even think, Fifty-Seven reached for the tranquilizer gun and shot the worker directly in his arm. He fell to the floor, knocked out, *unconscious.*

"Go! Push the button, dammit!" she yelled.

Right. The button. It was now exposed in all its glory. I reached over and pushed the red top. A slight ding indicated that it worked—that the barricade had been deactivated.

Even though the worker had only been awake for a few seconds, that was just enough time for him to call for help. Flashing red alarms suddenly went off throughout the entire facility. The words "code yellow" repeated over on a loop on the public address system.

"That son of a bitch. We have to go … *now*," urged Fifty-Seven.

I said no more. I gave the red button a final smash with the brick, breaking it into pieces. We were at a full sprint within seconds.

Left foot.

Right foot.

Cubicles and desks, tables and chairs, steel doors and machines—every object was a blur from the corner of my eyes. Fifty-Seven ran with the worker's tranquilizer gun. I dropped the brick, and we fled Z5.

The lobby was no safer than the sectors. Red lights illuminated the darkened hallways. Blaring sirens and sounds reverberated throughout every room. It felt like we were on display for every worker to see. Nevertheless, we ran.

Left foot.

Right foot.

Left foot.
Right foot.
Heels clicked against heels. Breathing slowly faltered. Reality became a blur, a twister, a dizzying cyclone of sorts. My stress intensified as I caught a glimpse of shadowy figures in the distance, emerging from behind like a group of stampeders charging after us. Whether a hallucination or not, it didn't matter. I moved faster, navigated more assuredly. My raging confidence and feelings of freedom and longing fueled my crazed mind. *Family. Home. Escape. Family. Home. Escape.* Thoughts of home motivated me to push forward.

Fifty-Seven kept a steady pace beside me. She mirrored my actions—the rise and fall of my feet as they landed on the ground, my posture and position, the way I held myself up when I ran. Her equal determination and confidence to escape made me wonder what her motives were. *What life will she be returning to? What drives her? What pushes her to keep going? Is there anything besides the line between life and death, or does she simply want to leave in order to be given a second chance and to get another opportunity to be free?* No, there was something else. Beneath her façade had to lie an *ulterior motive.*

We ran through the lobby. Footsteps and shouts were now more apparent and increasing in intensity. Workers with whistles and megaphones. Workers with weapons and restraints. Luckily, they weren't close enough yet to do anything to us. Their voices and yells fell on deaf ears. We continued to move ahead.

Left foot.
Right foot.
Left foot.
Right foot.

As we continued to pace forward, I quickly realized that we were at a disadvantage. The workers were much, *much* faster than we were. They were armed, experienced. All we had was a low-range tranquilizer gun. Nonetheless, Fifty-Seven and I were still in the lead. It was the result of the one thing they never had—a head start. And we were winning, beating them at their own twisted game, because in the end, they never even knew we had the guts to play. The irony made me laugh.

Finally, we reached the end of the lobby. The hum of the conveyer belts rattled me to my core as we exited Headquarters.

Left foot.

Right foot.

Two left turns. That's all it took to get to the stairway. I practically skipped the whole way there. Fifty-Seven held her breath. Just one more left turn until we'd get to see if my plan actually worked. I tensed up. The air became colder and thinner. Walls felt like they were closing in. Just a few more steps.

It is open. No metal barricade blocked the way. No security guards stood watch. The entrance to the stairs was completely clear, free for anybody to step through. Just four flights up to the doors to the exit. Beyond that was my home. Freedom. *Escape.*

I ran like never before.

Left foot.

Right foot.

The stairway was dark. Ominous shadows blanketed the landings in sheets of black as I went up two steps at a time. My feet thumped with every violent movement. The ground shook. Fifty-Seven followed. Laborious breaths rattled in my chest.

The alarms from the lobby below became fainter the higher up we got. Workers wearing boots and high heels created loud thumping noises upon running up the stairs behind us. I simply ignored them. Each floor passed in a blur until suddenly, the stairs ended. There were no more landings or railings or looping steps. I was on the fourth floor, the *Entryway*.

"Hey! Stop right there! Don't you dare move."

It was him. The almighty security guard of the facility. The very same guard who held the keys to the exit.

A red laser beam from his weapon illuminated on my chest. I was trapped, busted. My plan was ruined. There was nowhere to run, nowhere to hide. All I could do was turn myself in. I was completely frozen.

Suddenly, a familiar voice rang out from behind me.

"Fuck off you bastard!"

It all happened instantly. A tranquilizer dart shot right at the guard's face. He dropped to the floor unconscious within seconds.

"Now, now, you didn't think I'd just turn back around and leave you here alone, did you?"

How many times is this now that Fifty-Seven has saved my ass?

She stood over the guard's limp body like a heroic figure. We were actually going to get out. "C'mon, get your ass over here and help me find the keys!" she yelled.

I snapped out of my trance and rushed to her side, crouching down to floor-level. We both searched his keyring frantically. The sounds of workers' footsteps became louder and louder as they ran up the stairs.

"Here, try this one!" I exclaimed. It was golden, and the hue and shine perfectly matched the lock.

"On it," she said.

Fifty-Seven took it from my hands and approached the door. The workers got closer. She placed the key inside the lock, and to our surprise, it fit like a glove. We both held our breath. She slowly turned it until we heard a faint click, and after a few shakes, it was off.

Footsteps inched closer up the stairs. We both grabbed the handles of the large doors.

"On the count of three," Fifty-Seven began. "One."

"Two."

"*Three*," we said in unison.

We pulled with all our strength. Beyond the walls, freedom would be waiting. Our homes. Our *lives*. I got into a runner's position. We were both prepared to book it. The exit was right in front of our eyes as the doors finally opened big and wide. Except the other side wasn't what we expected. There were no trees or fields of grass, no oceans or bodies of water, no clear blue skies or gray clouds.

It was a concrete wall. From top to bottom, head to toe—a block of solid cement. And then it dawned on us.

There is no escape.

We are locked in.

I fell to my knees. The workers caught up to us. A tranquilizer dart hit me in my arm as the world turned pitch black. It was all over.

We failed.

CHAPTER 10

I opened my eyes to the abyss of a blackened room. My head throbbed with a rhythmic pounding while every fiber of my being ached with an uncontrollable pain. Machines filled up every corner of the space as neon blue lights and screens flashed in my eyes. A large device stationed at the front projected numbers, charts, and statistics, yet I couldn't read or make out what anything said. Blurry lines and patches of static blocked my vision. I couldn't explain it, but something about me had changed. The old Stella Winterfield was gone, instead replaced with a more fixed, *modified* version. I craned my neck to look around and came to a horrible realization. The machines and gadgets were all hooked up to *me*. I was propped up on a leather chair with a wire fastened around my waist. Muffled screams were all that could be mustered from my vocal cords as my teeth clamped down onto a mouth restraint. I was trapped, caged like a wild animal—a *failure*.

My memory slowly returned with every passing second as prior events replayed themselves in my head. I had been trying to escape. There was a lot of running and loud noises as I sprinted through a narrow hallway, up a flight of stairs. A girl was beside me. *Fifty-Seven*. Images of her face flashed throughout my mind. *What happened to her? Did they take her as well? Or did she just rat me out in order to get off the hook?* Whatever the case, she had been with me, attempting to break out. We had made it up four flights of stairs—all the way to the fourth floor, the Entryway. A guard pointed his gun at me, but Fifty-Seven swooped in to help, knocking him out. We both approached his unconscious body and immediately began looking for keys. I found the right one. We used it to remove the lock. The doors had opened, and then, *nothing*—a solid concrete wall. There was no exit. Escape was never an option. All along, the door had been a fake, a set-up, because if people had known there was no way out, they would've rebelled. But since it simply *existed*, everyone thought they were safe, that even if things went south, the exit would be tucked away in the back of their minds, giving them some form of reassurance and hope. It was a lie, all of it—always had been.

I was extremely fatigued. Just looking around the room intensified the throbbing in my head. Everything was spinning, yet closing my eyes only made the dizziness worse.

But my survival instincts kicked in. I thrashed around in the leather chair, kicking and screaming, attempting to slither my way out of the restraints. Metal chains and ropes violently scratched at my arms, making them bleed dark red. The cuts closed within seconds, yet a burning sensation permanently stung at my skin. Out of nowhere, a loud beeping noise, almost like an alarm, sounded from one of the machines, doubled with a blinking green light. I continued to struggle against the harness.

In almost an instant, a worker abruptly entered the room, followed by a strong burning odor.

"Aww, hello there! I see you've finally awoken! It only took you fourteen days," she chirped.

Fourteen days, exactly two weeks. Which meant I only had twenty days left before my inevitable demise. I tried to speak but struggled against the mouth restraint. All that came out were inaudible sounds.

"Oh, I'm sorry. Let me take that out for you," she teased.

As soon as she removed the guard, I screamed for my life. I cried for help, in the hopes that anybody would hear me. As expected, my irrational idea wasn't of any use.

"You can stop screaming. There's no one here that can help you," she cooed. Her voice was like blood red velvet that flowed like honey, evil and alluring—like a siren tricking a sailor on the open sea. My yells died down as I quickly realized she was right. Nobody was coming to save me.

"Now that we got that out of the way, let's try this again! Hi, my name is Dr. Scarlet Adams. Okay, now it's your turn!"

I tried being defiant. Maybe if I didn't answer her silly questions, she'd just give up and stop asking. So, I remained silent.

"Oh, so you're not talkative now, huh? Well, the longer you keep your mouth shut, the more time you waste," she said.

"Stella."

"That's more like it! Hello, Stella! Now, before we continue with anything else, I must ask you a few mandatory questions," Scarlet began. "First, let me ask, what exactly were you doing After Hours with Fifty-Seven that was so important?"

"Sleepwalking," I responded.

"Oh… that's funny because a few nights before, it appears you also happened to be sleepwalking! We dismissed it as you being sick, which it turns out, you were. But it says here that you passed the sickness testing and were released from the infirmary not long after. So, let me ask you again. What were you doing After Hours with Fifty-Seven?" Her tone became more serious as her demeanor abruptly changed.

"Nothing."

"Very well then. You asked for it."

Almost instantly, an electric shock flowed throughout my entire body. Piercing sensations burned my skin and left me feeling dazed and dehydrated, worsening my already weakened state.

"Every time you refuse to tell the truth, I'll increase the shock levels on the machine. Now please, answer the fucking question."

I gave up. I was weak. A part of me wanted to believe this was all a dream, that I would wake up back in my bedroom at home. But I knew deep down, this was very real.

"We were … trying to escape. I wanted to get … to the exit." My breathing was labored and quick, making it difficult to speak.

"Oh? And why would you want to do that?" Scarlet perked up.

"I don't … want to die. Your people … kill."

"Oh honey. My people don't kill anyone. We simply guide you to the next stage of your existence. Think of it like you're already dead."

Her words were like riddles, twisting mysteries for my brain.

"Am I … dead?"

She paused. "It depends. Do you feel dead?"

"I don't … know."

"Well then, you have no reason to be upset! We *saved* you, Stella, saved you from that sick and twisted life. Now you get to spend the rest of that life with *us*." Scarlet gently caressed my face while cupping my head in her hands, shaking it back and forth in a menacingly playful manner. "Your participation has allowed us to make technological advancements like never before! Just think, we give you a nice home, food, and an education. So why? Why would you ever want to leave? You help us and we help you in return. Forget about this whole life-death dilemma. That's something you will *never* have to worry about again. I promise."

As she moved her face closer to mine, her breath smelled heavily of cheap mints and coffee. Just observing her mannerisms, looking at all the features on her face, made me sick to my stomach. Sure, nearly all of the workers in the facility came off in a bad way, as they were either too fake or too odd. But Scarlet—she was a worker like no other—a true super villain. From her strangely seductive voice to her evil demeanor, I wouldn't wish for my worst enemy to cross her path.

"Anyway, now that I'm done ranting, we have more important matters to discuss. I'm sure you've noticed that you're in someplace ... different. These are the Experimentation Cells. It's where we take all the naughty children and do extraordinary extensive research on them as punishment! Isn't that fun?"

My face contorted in disgust. "If you want to keep doing research, then how come your people don't just experiment on everyone?" It was easier to talk now, partially because of my newfound rage.

"Don't be silly! If we did experiments on everyone, then they wouldn't trust us, now would they?" Scarlet said.

So that's what this was to them: a game of trust and manipulation. But unlike everybody else who conformed to their standards, followed their orders like lost puppies, I was able to see through their bullshit and lies, me and Fifty-Seven both.

They weren't able to trick us, yet they still somehow held all the power. Now here I was, hanging on by a thread of dignity. No amount of confidence would ever be strong enough to break me out of this tethered chair.

"Anywho, as I was saying… this is your Experimentation Cell. We brought you here the night of your attempted breakout, and for the past fourteen days, we have been performing tests and experiments specifically correlated to you. Thankfully, you were asleep through all of it… those drugs really hit you hard! But unfortunately, I can't say the same for your friend."

Fifty-Seven! So, they did capture her.

"What the hell did you do? What type of screwed up experiments did you do on her?" I raised my voice slightly above a yell.

"Don't worry. Just the same type of stuff. However, it was a bit of an … uncomfortable process. You'll see what I mean soon enough," she said through clenched teeth.

"See what you mean? Don't you dare try that shit on me!"

Scarlet sighed and put on another one of her malicious smiles. "Unfortunately, it is just company policy. Every subject that we bring to the Experimentation Cells is required to stay for fifteen days of trials. You're just a little bit below the mark. Today will be your last round of lab testing, whereafter you will then be transferred to another wonderful place, my personal favorite! It's called the DOD, which stands for 'Direct Order Dormitory,' but instead, I prefer to call it the Dungeons of Doom! Quite fitting. You'll be required to stay there for another ten days… oh, but don't worry! Half of your time there will be occupied with drug-induced sleep."

I balled my fists and stared at her. "Who *are* you? All of you? Why are you doing this? Why did you put a chip in my head?"

"Because, Stella… we're going to be the ones to save the world."

Suddenly, with a wave of her hands, Dr. Adams pulled down a metal lever on the wall. It made a horrible screeching sound, as if it were thousands of years old. Upon flipping the switch, the lights on my chair lit up in shades of neon blue and teal. A chirping sound, like crickets, softly hummed in the background. Everything began to buzz and vibrate in a constant state of motion while the woman before me pulled up a screen etched with different markings, charts, and numbers. As if on cue, a metal gadget, like a cap, craned down to where it fit on my head. The negatively charged electrons made my hair frizz up and stick to the top of the device, like rubbing a balloon against a carpet.

"One of the final areas we test is your brain. Now, I'd say you won't be able to feel a thing, but unfortunately, that's not true! Our funding doesn't really focus on the wellness of our subjects. Then again, you're not going to remember this in a few weeks from now, anyway, so who cares?"

The buzzing of the machines drowned out most of the sounds in the room, yet Scarlet's obnoxious voice never ceased to go below a whisper in my mind.

"Before we begin, do you have anything you'd like to say? Speaking may be a bit difficult after this," she asked.

As she rested her hands atop the activation button of the device, there was only one thing I could possibly think of. My words didn't mean much anymore, but I wanted to hit her where it hurt, say something that would really leave a mark. I pursed my lips and shut my eyes, as if she were just a monster under my bed.

"I hope your parents are proud of you."

And then, the entire world as I saw it *changed*. Flashing blue and white lights consumed my vision. Cerulean walls almost sparkled amid the electric shocks as energy-sucking, life-altering powers emitted from the base of the machine. My brain felt like it was being fried, as if it were nothing but a plate of eggs over a stove. Every bone and muscle of my being shook uncontrollably under the pressure, as the room began transforming in unnatural ways. Walls stretched and compressed. The ceiling spun in a constant state of rotation, counterclockwise, 360 degrees. I was pulled into a portal from the head down, or at least that's how I felt. The gurgling sound as I choked on my own spit was enough to make anyone pass out. And then there was Scarlet. Her outlined figure stood poised in front of a large screen as it changed every second, projecting data specific to me. As I experienced that intense pain, she simply clicked her acrylic nails together and marveled at the magnificence of their technological advancements. My test results were like bags of gold falling right into her grubby hands.

Finally, after what felt like ten agonizing minutes, the machines turned off. All energy in the room ceased; the buzzing of electricity and vibrations died down. As my vision slowly returned and the aftereffects began to kick in, Scarlet waved her hands in front of my face. She wore that ever-so-familiar, gut wrenching, stupid smile, a look I wish I could wipe away with a single swipe.

"Yoo-hoo! Earth to Stella!" she cheered. After a while, I gave in to her antics and readjusted my eyes to where they met hers.

"There you are! Your tests are finally done! I would tell you 'good job' or something, but you were only conscious for one of them, so you really didn't do anything at all. But that wasn't so bad, right? I hope you understand how much your great efforts have allowed this facility to grow and expand."

I tuned her out. She was all faux niceties and back-handed compliments, a bunch of junk that I didn't want to hear in my permanently scarred state. However, I never got to see her reaction to my parting comment. It was an impulse decision, one that I'd wanted to say for the longest time upon arriving here. *"I hope your parents are proud of you."*

As if she were reading my mind, Dr. Adams suddenly had a shift in demeanor. Her tone became more high-pitched, as if she had something to hide. And then, she hit me with an unexpected revelation.

"Since you had ever the interest in my parents, I would like to tell you something. They are *extremely* proud of me, Stella. For all they know, I'm working at a highly prestigious company, risking my life every day to fulfill my duties. Nobody is aware of what's happening behind these closed doors. They only know what the media tells them, or rather, what *we* tell the media to tell them. In fact, our work is so confidential that there is only a 1% hire rate in our organization, and the only people who have ever seen the inside of our building are our employees. So, yes. It is an honor to be working here." There it was, the true secrecy of this whole operation. I just couldn't see the point.

"Anyway, enough small talk. It's time for you to be transferred! This is my favorite part of the agenda, where I get to take you to the Dungeons of Doom! Well, really the Direct Order Dormitory, but that's far less fun to say. Now, no more chitchat. Let's get on with it." Scarlet foamed at the mouth. Just the thought of keeping me locked up brought her joy—a true sociopath.

Finally, I was released from the shackles and restraints of the leather chair. It was strange getting back on my feet again, having control over my own body, although the feelings were short-lived as Scarlet pushed and pulled me along, dragging me by the wrist. The supposed Dungeons of Doom didn't sound too appealing, but the thought of actually having freedom of mobility kept me going. Not to mention the growing hunger pain that stirred in my belly. Now I'd get a bed (or cot) and a quick meal to satisfy my stomach.

The walk there was long and arduous. Dr. Adams shoved me forward, prompting me to move faster. After some time, we stopped at an ominous staircase. The odors that wafted from the bottom reeked of swamp water and sweat.

"Just below these steps will be your new room for the next ten days. Exciting, yes?" she chirped.

I simply responded with an unenthusiastic hum.

As we traversed farther down, the air became murkier, more humid, and I regretted ever following through with the procedure. Scarlet stopped upon a large metal door. It contained locks and handles of every kind. She swiftly took out a silver key, used it to unbolt the locks, and the door to the room opened, revealing a depressing space.

"Enjoy! You'll get food twice a day, and someone will occasionally come by to check up on you, but besides that, you're on your own. Goodbye, Stella!" And with that, she closed the door, locking it up behind her, trapping me inside.

The room was no better than the Experimentation Cell. A stiff cot was in the right corner, held up by a metal frame with a rock-hard mattress. Corroded walls of cement were cracked up, and the ceiling was discolored with blotchy patches of mold. Small flecks of ash and dust fell from the floor-to-ceiling picture window, allowing spots of faux sunlight to illuminate the center of the gloomy chamber and cast shadows throughout. A shelf of books, along with a sink, were next to the bed, deteriorating from lack of proper care, and a dripping tap made slow pitters in the corner, collecting from a leak up above.

I was done, weak, defeated. Carefully, I staggered over to the cot, and for the first time in three weeks, I cried. *What did I do to deserve this fate? Why is this happening to me?* Over and over, I cried, wondered, and screamed helplessly into the pillow until I fell asleep.

CHAPTER
UNKNOWN: PART 3

FIFTY-SEVEN

Fifty-Seven was tired—tired of the Experimentation Cell, tired of the facility. After waking up on day six of the testing procedures, she was worn down and weak. Now, as she sat on the stiff cot in the DOD, she wondered why she was even here. Her life and relationships were taken away and replaced by numbers and statistics. She wasn't Fifty-Seven. She wasn't a lab rat. She was simply herself—*Elliana Jones*. A name that had been removed and forgotten in the abyss of time.

Flashes of bits and pieces of her memory seemed to be coming back to her slowly but surely. Elliana remembered leaving a perfume store, and her next stop was the food court. Except on the way there, everything changed. Loud sirens erupted from every corner, and people ran in all directions, screaming for their lives. She stood amid it all like a deer in the headlights, her body frozen with fear. She couldn't get herself to physically move. Eventually, her survival instincts kicked in, and she ran for the mall exit.

Then the explosion happened.

Before passing out and being brought to the facility, Elliana had attempted to rescue a young blonde-haired girl who had been caught in the explosion. She was unsuccessful as the girl died soon afterward.

Ash and rubble, dust and debris, destruction and demolition—it was everywhere. The once lively mall with bustling customers had been torn apart. Burning red flames set fire to the building and emitted plumes of black smoke, covering people in coats of gray. Bodies littered the floor like trash—some dead, some unconscious—while medics arrived on the scene instantly to attend to the injured. Two large ambulances sped up into the parking lot. Their sirens were loud and dreadful, screaming above the flurry and chaos of the tragedy.

After that was hazy, and the next thing she could remember was being snatched up and forced to go to sleep. Then she woke up in one of the facility's labs on the gurney in the center of the room.

"Okay, I'm identifying Elliana Jones, seventeen years old, et cetera, et cetera. She was the fifty-seventh member, last person to transfer," she heard one of the doctors announce.

The other doctors in the room hurriedly typed on laptops, sending, and receiving information.

"Can we get a time on that?" a second doctor asked.

"Fetching that right now," responded a third. "Alright, I got the info. It says here it took her fifty minutes to cross."

As they clicked away on their devices, Elliana gave a soft sigh. While doctors one and two didn't realize what was happening, the third became very startled. "Hey guys, come quick. She's waking up!"

"What do you mean?" the second asked. But when he looked up from his work, he noticed it as well. Fifty-Seven was very much conscious, blankly staring at the men around her.

"Shit, drug her up. Get one of the cloths!" he urged.

"On it, boss."

Effortlessly, the doctor fetched one of the strips and handed it to his coworker. He brought it up to Elliana's mouth and knocked her unconscious, sending her into another drug-like slumber.

But, before she was completely knocked out, she heard them say, "Damn it, do you think she'll remember?"

"No, this Memorant is strong. It'll keep her memories at bay."

And through it all, she and Forty-Eight had devised plan after plan to attempt an escape, but all proved to be fruitless. The two never were able to succeed. After trying for the second time, she and Forty-Eight were caught for good. The last thing she remembered before collapsing to the ground that day was simply staring at the exit, the concrete wall, the cage. That's all they were—*caged animals*—and this time, she had proof. Escaping was impossible.

When she opened her eyes six days later—and oh, what a horrible sight—she was strapped into a leather chair while workers and scientists ran tests on her. They typed notes onto their laptops, jotted down sketches in their journals, all while laughing and smiling like sociopaths. The discomfort was unbearable as strange sensations jolted through her body like electricity. All she could think about was what they did to Forty-Eight.

"I see. She possesses different qualities than our other subjects. Maybe it has something to do with her mother, yet there's no way to prove that for sure," one of the workers rambled on. They didn't even notice she was awake.

The days were indistinguishable as minutes morphed into hours and constant pain affected her ability to think. Yet before she knew it, the workers unstrapped her from the chair, speaking some nonsense about a DOD. Elliana didn't know what it meant, but she didn't care. She was finally free from all the trials and tortuous experiments.

The place she was brought was like that of a jail cell. Gray, concrete walls, a rusted cot, and all the necessities. Although the bed was firm and not at all like a soft mattress, she was too tired to care. As soon as her head hit the rough pillow, she immediately fell into a deep sleep, getting some well-deserved rest.

After some time, Elliana woke up on her cot feeling terribly sick and malnourished. A plate of food sat on the floor, untouched and waiting to be eaten. Without giving it a second thought, she picked it up and ate the contents with her bare hands.

She was not a number. She was not a statistic. Instead, she was simply herself. Her name wasn't Fifty-Seven, no. It was, and always had been…

…Elliana Jones.

CHAPTER 11

It was day eight within the Dungeons of Doom. Most of my time was spent either sleeping or reading books. Often, a worker would appear with a plate of food and urge me to eat, although I rarely ever did. Just forty-eight more hours within this wretched cell—that's all I had to endure.

As I sat upright on the cot admiring the floor-to-ceiling picture window, all I could think about was my home—how badly I wanted to be in the comfortable confinement of those blue plaster walls, feeling my family's warm embrace. Those distant dreams were the only thoughts that motivated me.

Suddenly, something changed. My head pounded as the floor shook beneath my feet. I buckled under the pressure and fell to the ground, hitting the solid concrete landing. Colors and lights flickered and flashed within my eyes, making the room spin around in circles like a carnival ride. My fragile body felt as if it was breaking into fractured pieces, my guts exploding from the inside out. *This is it*, I thought. *The world is finally ending.*

I closed my eyes in anticipation, ducked beneath the cot, and covered my small frame. The pain was unbearable. Objects melted into each other to transform the world around me until I couldn't discern one thing from another. Everything was a blur of shapes, and lights, and sounds, and items, and feelings, and senses as I fell deeper into the core of my mind. Reality was unrealistic, life was unlively, and my human body was unhuman. The skin of me, Stella Winterfield, ripped apart, while everything I came to know about the facility disappeared. The chamber was gone, nothing but an empty vortex of space-time, and I could only wonder when this nightmare was going to end.

And then, as soon as it had begun, all the sensations ceased. The floor stopped rumbling, and the pounding in my head died down. I waited anxiously—for what, I didn't know. Nonetheless, it was over.

Or so I thought.

As I opened my eyes to re-enter the DOD, I quickly realized that something was very off. My small chamber was gone— the cot, the sink, the bookshelf. Instead, I was strapped onto a chair, unable to move. A large screen stretching for miles blinked with thousands of codes, constantly changing, as a red flashing light sent alarms throughout the room. Meanwhile, the words "System Error" flashed amid technological devices and created vibrations that made the ground shake. However, as I closely observed my surroundings, my heart instantly dropped. It was a sickening sight, and I could barely process what I was looking at.

All of us, people from the facility for as far as the eye could see, were passed out on mechanical chairs. Numbers labeled the sides which identified who we were. Two spots away from me sat Fifty. She, along with everyone else, was completely unconscious, bound to the machine by two wires connected to her forehead. A horrible realization dawned upon me as I observed rows upon rows of people: Thirty-One, Sixty-Four, Fifteen, *Fifty-Seven*. I tried to move, but then saw that I, too, was connected by the wires. And so, I did the only thing I could—*scream*.

"Hey, wake the hell up! None of that shit is real. We're being brainwashed!" I shouted as loudly as I could, but my plea was just a whisper compared to the wail of the sirens.

"Can you hear me? I said wake up!"

I continued to yell until a group of workers quickly rushed inside the room. Their voices were hushed and frantic, and I couldn't make out a thing they were saying. I locked eyes with a young man, and his expression changed to one of pure terror. In an instant, he and another female worker sped over to me, maneuvering through the countless other unconscious bodies.

"How the hell did this happen? And what are we going to tell the boss, dammit?" the man hollered.

"It was a chip malfunction. Connect her back into the system!"

"I'm trying, I'm trying! All her programs are down."

"Oh, son of a... these wires are disconnected."

"Then connect them! She's already been conscious for too long."

That was the last thing I heard before I passed out. As the woman fixed the machine, a white jolt of energy rushed through my veins like electricity. Before I knew it, the world transformed once more as images of the DOD morphed back in front of my eyes.

Regaining my vision, I noticed that I was still crouched underneath the cot as if nothing had ever happened. Life was still and motionless, the silence was like music to my ears, but that moment of peace didn't last very long. Immense fear took over my senses as the severity of my current situation hit me like a ton of bricks. I tried brushing it off, tried convincing myself that what I saw wasn't real, like a child just finding out about Santa. Maybe it was all an elaborate dream or some strange hallucination caused by lack of sleep. But in the end, nothing could explain what had happened. It was the truth behind the lies. The man behind the curtain.

I was overwhelmed. My perspective on the facility changed as I desperately tried to figure out what I saw. The large screen of code, rows of people passed out—it all rubbed me the wrong way. So, to calm myself down, I eventually decided to read a book. The selection was limited, but it got me through the ordeal of my current situation. As I rummaged through the stacks of neatly placed novels and colorful kid's stories, I came across something new, something unusual. It was discreetly shoved behind every other book in a way that made it appear someone hid it there, only for me to discover. It was titled *Life Within a Coma*. The cover was old and torn, but each letter shone with a gold finish while dust collected on the spine and in between every off-white page. It looked ancient, untouched, as if it had been sitting there for years. My heart began to race as I held the journal in my hands, the edges of the pages covered in a shiny coat. They reflected against the lights and sparkled like beautiful stars.

This can't be real? This has to be a setup!

But what if it's not?

What if this is my ticket?

Curious, I flipped to the first section and started reading.

PROPERTY OF DRYSTAN MARWOOD.

The following is the first-hand account of my research—everything leading up to the events of the development, concept, and construction of all aspects of the facility. It is a case study of life, death, and everything in between.

I created MLD as a haven for afterlife research, but more importantly, immortality. It has been scientists' main goal for decades now; however, I'm proud to say that I've brought the world a step closer. What started off as a simple project has advanced to offices and buildings all around the world where countless professionals collect data on what we know about death itself.

In my area of expertise, I often visit local hospitals and observe the patients who are in comatose states. No matter the cause or reason, I conduct experiments on as many individuals as possible. Just recently, I've developed and tested the first ever model of my new machine known as Comatiz, an advanced technological device which allows its user to fall into a regulated coma. With this invention, I've been able to choose test subjects for my latest psychological experiments regarding what happens when a person enters a deep state of unconsciousness. I am now ready to begin my first round of clinical trials.

JANUARY 15, 1985

Today began the first hands-on experiment which involved coma activity. I assembled a group of three vastly different test subjects: Brody Courtez (fifteen-year-old male), Evalie Armani (thirty-two-year-old female), and Lilla Smith (six-year-old female). I set up a Comatiz machine and tested one person at a time. Then, for each subject, I performed different trials to see how their three senses reacted to external forces. My first test involved sense of smell where I brought out samples of artificial fragrances and sprayed them around the room. The second was a hearing test. I placed a pair of headphones on the subject and played various sounds, such as wildlife ambience, rain, and laughing. Finally, the last test was my personal favorite: a sight game. For this, I strapped a headset on the volunteer and projected various images. Once all the simulations were complete, I then turned off Comatiz to wake up the individuals and quiz them on the things they saw or experienced during their time in the coma.

I collected my data and found multiple patterns across all subjects. When presented with a smell, sight, or sound, that recognition often transferred over to their consciousness. For example, if they were shown an image of a blue house while in the coma, their conscious minds would "travel" as if they were standing directly in front of it. Furthermore, anything that they *experienced outside was incorporated directly into their in-between state. This means that although their bodies were in my office, their minds were someplace else, and my simulations shaped those imaginary worlds.*

I can conclude from this study that what occurs during a coma is unidentifiable and, overall, unpredictable. But when presented with a test variable or other stimulating source, like sounds and images, the subject's point of view becomes altered. This is a powerful new discovery that I believe can advance my immortality research, and I'm excited to see where my experiments will take me next.

My eyes skimmed over every word, and I absorbed the information like a human sponge. That burning curiosity never extinguished but grew like a raging fire. And so, I voraciously read through each section with heightened motivation, jumping from page to page as if it were my life's mission.

FEBRUARY 6, 1985

Today I tested my first prototype of the Facility Simulation. According to the results of my experiments, when shown a projected image while in a coma, a subject will be placed within the setting where that image takes place. For example, if a desert scene is presented, the minds of those who are unconscious will inadvertently "travel" to that same desert. After my trials on January 15, I decided to take it a step further by not only using pictures during these tests, but rather "subconscious programming." It is a new concept I created that modifies the minds of the humans who undergo the Comatiz operation.

Subconscious programming is accomplished by strapping subjects into a machine and sending lines of code directly to their brains. To perform a regulated coma, we need to use my specialized technology: two suctioned wires attached to the user's forehead, a metal cap used to conduct the electrical waves a metal cap used to conduct the electrical waves of the brain and allow the chip to be implanted, as well as the remote that activates the device. I developed the final version of this machine in November 1984. When pressing the button on the control panel, the energy from the wires grows exponentially until the body cracks under the pressure, eventually causing the subject to pass out. Well, with my newly updated research, I've discovered a way to transfer coding scripts through the ends of those wires, thus sending a program right into the subject's mind. I began working on a system with basic commands as well as building the digital construction of my latest and greatest creation: the Facility. Written in the code are attributes and functions of a high-tech laboratory. It's the meeting place for all of my subjects. I like to think of it as home base. Within its parameters are properties and applications like none before—things such as quick healing and advanced weapons, like tranquilizer darts which cause memory loss. But of course, these *are just my brainstorming ideas. I will soon begin building a physical model of what the Facility could one day look like, both here on Earth and where my comatose test subjects will reside.*

I skipped ahead toward the end of the book. Countless pages of graphs, sketches, and sloppy notes filled the journal up to the brim. I wanted to put it down, but my heart couldn't take it. That burning curiosity brought me over the edge and created a weird sense of rage from deep within.

OCTOBER 4, 1994

Finally, after ten years of programming, modeling, and perfecting my work, it is complete: the Facility Simulation. Upon undergoing the Comatiz process, a subject's consciousness will now be transferred to my digital building. This will be referred to as the crossing. Its duration will vary but will be long enough for a behavior modification chip to be implanted into the subject's head behind the pupils. Once this is complete, the subject will stay in a place known as the in-between. The building itself will consist of four floors with over 200 different sectors. The sectors labeled will be different areas of study, ranging from A-0.5, the place where the subjects are sent to die, all the way up to sector Z9, also known as the Exit. Although the facility is boarded up with fake doors and entryways, that room is the true way out. It's a secret area meant for the workers only, where a Comatiz machine is set up in the middle of the room along with all its proper tools. The facility is equipped with all the essentials: classrooms, dormitories, offices, and new inventions such as ElastaGlass and Memorant.

ElastaGlass appears to be a holographic material, yet upon making contact with human skin, it shifts and bends in unimaginable ways. It's what we'll use in order to track every subject's fingerprints, brain activity, and genetic makeup. Meanwhile, Memorant is a strong drug which workers will inject into the new facility patients to sedate them and wipe their memories. It can also be found in the tranquilizer darts as a disciplinary measure, affecting its user by making them forget the previous four minutes of their life. A larger dose can be injected directly into the patient if a longer duration of memory loss is necessary.

My script includes thousands of lines of information and code which outline all the features and regulations of the facility, and I couldn't feel more accomplished with my progress. This has been the biggest step for MLD by far, and I can't wait to see how our research expands.

JANUARY 5, 1995

As MLD continues to grow, I started my own side project that could exponentially advance my company's work. Introducing the Immortality Pact: an organization which helps fund immortality research. For every subject that dies after *forty days in the facility, we'll receive a monetary bonus which will help fund afterlife studies.*

I flipped to the very end of the book. Hundreds of diary entries filled each page from top to bottom, and needless to say, I was captivated. Finally, I reached the last entry.

MARCH 3, 1999

And so, I've reached the last page in my journal. It's been a pleasure conducting this research, working with fellow friends, and doing a job I absolutely love. Hopefully, in the future, every person on Earth will have achieved immortality (thanks to MLD and the sacrifices made along the way). We are changing history, revolutionizing the modern-day world with our extraordinary technological masterpieces. I am the proud CEO and boss of the Mid-Life Death Corp, the accomplished creator of the Facility Simulation, and the distinguished organizer of the Immortality Pact Organization. I, Doctor Drystan Marwood, am the next hero of our generation, the next hero of the world.

I closed the book after reading that final sentence. Everything about it fascinated yet disgusted me at the same time. I couldn't help but feel like I had lost to these people, that I'd fallen for their silly tricks. This entire time, I've just been asleep in a coma, completely unconscious?

I began to piece things together—the strange midday nightmare, the one with the blackened room and screens of code, and *the fact that there was no escape*. However, that's where I was wrong. There *was* an escape, only it wasn't physical. I needed to wake myself up. Because that *was* no nightmare. I was awake. *Disconnected from the machine*!

Not all hope was lost. There was a future for me and Fifty-Seven. We just couldn't give up—not yet at least! For the first time in a while, I actually smiled.

Finally, for once, there was hope for something good.

CHAPTER 12

It was my last day in the dungeons. I woke up to the sound of the cell door opening loudly—every metal chain clanging and hitting one another. The lock clicked open, and the faintest of light filtered into the room as an elderly man wearing a formal suit stood in front of the entrance, guarded by two masked workers. The strong stench of his cologne wafted inside. He had an intimidating energy, one of an all-mighty god who ruled over his servants or a fire whose ashes burned like the blackest night. Meanwhile, his hazel eyes reflected colors of blazing red as if he were nothing but a robot running on a list of commands. The two people beside him sported gray blindfolds, their eyes covered by dark cloth. It was a very unsettling scene.

"Forty-Eight, your stay at the Direct Order Dormitory has ended. Please follow me." His voice was hoarse, yet grand as it echoed throughout the hallways.

I rose from the cot, and it squeaked and rattled with my every movement. My feet hit the cold floor, chilling every bone in my body from the ground up. The masked workers moved out of the way, creating a path for us both to walk through.

"Forty-Eight, I have already met you, but you have not met me. I am Doctor Drystan Marwood, owner and creator of this very facility. Let me preface this by saying I did you a favor. It was a great honor to be brought here, so tell me… why did you try to escape?" he asked.

We slowly walked up the stairs, the atmosphere chilly and filled with a strange emptiness. *So, this was the infamous Dr. Marwood, the mastermind behind it all.*

"I don't know. I think I was brainwashed," I replied, playing an act. Maybe if I pretended like I had a change of heart, he would be more forgiving.

"Ah, but of course. Did somebody get in your head? Because I can assure you that we mean no harm at all."

He continued like this for a while, saying nice words and affirmations, doing just about anything to prove that he was the good guy. I just nodded and smiled, smiled and nodded. Until finally, we arrived at yet another office. I was getting sick of the same off-white rooms with large tables and desks, but alas, here I was again.

"Take a seat. I am required to ask you a set of questions before you are permitted to return to your dorm," Drystan informed.

That was all this place was. Offices, research, numbers, questions, and a never-ending cycle of bullshit. It was exhausting, time and time again, but I had to comply nonetheless. *Just doing what I have to do to survive.*

After I made myself comfortable, Dr. Marwood took out a clipboard and pen while crossing one leg over the other. Then, he cleared this throat and began writing.

"So, Forty-Eight. Can you tell me why you wanted to escape?" he started, glaring straight at me.

"I thought that this place was dangerous. It was my mistake," I replied, keeping up my fake persona.

"Very well. Now, you are aware that you broke rule four, act six, as well as rule seven, act five. It states in our conditions, under the fourth clause, that 'All workers must be respected; interacting with a worker in any way that harms or intends to harm, such as hitting, humiliating, pushing, touching, pinching, cutting, sabotaging, trapping, throwing objects at, spreading rumors, or using any sort of weapon that includes a knife, sharp edge or blade, injections, or a tranquilizer gun/tranquilizer darts, will be punished.' On the night of your attempted escape, you and Fifty-Seven used a tranquilizer gun to shoot at a security guard, causing him to pass out and experience memory loss. Now, some could argue that it was in self-defense; however, you did not have moral intentions and, instead, harmed the worker out of spite. Overall, his actions were correct, and you were not given permission to go about your act. Am I clear?"

"Yes, sir."

"Good. But unfortunately, you also broke rule seven. Under the seventh clause, it says, 'Do not question anything; those who are in opposition or denial of our actions and express those feelings in negative/impactful ways, such as making a scene or rally, boycotting, forming a protest or rivalry group, brainwashing others, openly badmouthing workers, leaving suspicious notes or cues, forming plans against our corporation, ideating/attempting escape, unlocking files/rooms/instruments/doors without permission, and documenting personal moments which invade privacy to use against our benefit will be punished.' You and Fifty-Seven fall under a few of these categories. That is unacceptable, and behaviors like these will not be allowed or tolerated. Do you understand?"

"Yes, sir."

"Excellent. Just sign these papers indicating that you understand the rules and regulations and promise to always comply with them. Failure to comply will result in greater punishment."

Drystan slid over the papers and handed me his pen, indicating the spot which I was supposed to sign. Sloppily, I wrote in big script, "48" on each sheet, proving my cooperation.

"Perfect! Now, before I send you on your way, there is one other minor issue I'd like to address," he said in an uneasy tone.

"What's that?" I asked.

"Well, you were only seventeen years old when you arrived here. However, today is your birthday, therefore making you eighteen, a legal adult. All adults, no matter the age, are given different accommodations. Instead of living in a dorm and having to take required classes, you will be trained to perform a specific job around the facility. And, instead of residing in Headquarters on floor one, you will be transferred to the Landing on floor two. We operate a bit differently in the adult world. There is no set schedule. Instead, you choose your own day-to-day activities. You'll only be expected to show up at a certain time for your training, usually ranging from one to two hours for a few days, and once that's done, you'll take shifts at your new job. The cafeteria is open whenever, so you can order what you want, when you want it. Also, the time for After Hours is extended. Instead of an eight o'clock curfew, you'll have until ten."

I was appalled, too stunned to speak. No more dorm? No more living in Headquarters? Just the thought made my heart sink into my stomach. The last thing I wanted to do was *work* for these people.

"I'm sorry, but you said I would be moved to floor two. Where will I stay? And will I still be able to visit the first floor?" I asked all at once.

"Yes, you'll move to floor two, the Landing, where you'll also be given a connected room, almost like a small house that you share. Now, when it comes to visiting floor one, it all depends. If you are selected for a job that's specifically stationed in Headquarters, you will go there for your daily shifts. However, if not, you won't have access to that level," he stated matter-of-factly.

I kept up my calm and collected façade, but on the inside, I was panicking. Having no more access to floor one meant no more access to Fifty-Seven, which meant no more chance of escape. Instead, I'd have to spend the rest of my ten days alive working as a trainee under a bunch of corrupted scientists. Having all this new information dumped on me out of nowhere was overwhelming. Nobody cared to give me a warning or tell me that my birthday was soon, and that I'd have to adjust to new living spaces and conditions. Then again, when have these people really told me anything about anything?

"So, does that mean the jobs are picked randomly?" I asked.

"Indeed."

I sat in silence for a few moments. Being transferred to the second floor would change the dynamic of everything. My situation just got way more complicated.

"Well, you are ready. Come along. Your new room is waiting," Drystan said, practically pushing me out of his office. I sulked the entire walk over. As it turned out, I had been on the third floor this entire time, a place called the Science Lab where they performed extensive tests on all the misbehavers.

Begrudgingly, I trudged down the staircase and arrived at a platform, the entrance to the Landing.

Left foot.

Right foot.

However, to my surprise, it was beautiful compared to Headquarters. Clean marble walls seemed to gleam from every corner while an abundance of healthy plants added contrast to the landscape. Blue furnishings and buzzing machines gave the lobby a sort of spark, along with the draping vines which dangled off wood slabs, complimenting sandpaper-colored walls and the occasional tan floorboard. Vibrancy made all the difference between the two worlds, and for a moment, I forgot that I was even in the facility. Fresh aromas of baked goods consumed my senses, as well as the light chatter of people who laughed and smiled. It was just like home. Dr. Marwood made a left, nearing uniform dorms that stood in perfectly symmetrical rows. Each one had a combination of numbers above their door, written in black calligraphy. Then, he stopped upon reaching room 102, gesturing toward the entryway.

"This is your new home! Your schedule and job should be waiting for you inside. Good luck, Forty-Eight," he said kindly before walking off. I was left standing in front of the baby blue building with plaster walls, *just like home*.

After discovering that the door was locked, I rapidly knocked multiple times until somebody answered. However, I wanted to throw up after seeing the girl on the other side. Split dyed hair of pink and platinum rested along her shoulders while bright blue eyes dully stared back at me. She was like an older manifestation of my sister. *Just like home*. I instantly brushed the thought aside and tried to keep my composure.

"Are you the last one?" she asked, looking me up and down.

"I'm sorry?" I said, taken aback.

"Like, the last roommate or whatever. There's three of us here already."

"I mean, I guess."

"Perfect! We've all been waiting for you," she chirped, stepping aside to let me pass. As I entered the building, two other girls, only one year older than me in appearance, sat around a mahogany table, intently staring at an envelope. They were in a kitchen, much larger than my previous dorm, which contained an oven, microwave, and full-sized fridge.

"Just a quick introduction: I'm Eighty-Six, to my left is Eighty-Eight, and to my right is Seventy-Three," she said, pointing to each girl. "I guess we all live together now. Since it's everyone's first day, that means we get assigned a job, and the selections are in that envelope. I thought it would be a good idea for us all to open it at the same time!"

Her enthusiasm was killing me. From the looks of it, I couldn't believe that it was only this girl's first day at the facility. How was she not terrified? How was she not confused?

Eighty-Six went up to the table and snatched the manilla envelope, twirling it around her fingers as if it were a toy.

"And of course, I'll be doing the honors!" she teased. "Here, sit down, uh…"

"Forty-Eight," I finished. "My name's Forty-Eight."

"Well quit standing around and join us!" Eighty-Six gestured, calling me over. "Now, on the count of three, I'm going to open the letter," she exclaimed, doing a soft drumroll on the table. "One… two… *three*."

The seal on the envelope practically ripped open under her sharp acrylic nails, revealing the piece of paper inside. Thin cursive writing neatly flowed on the page, covered top to bottom in words and sentences. I craned my neck from the opposite end of the table, scanning for my name and newly assigned job, my stomach tied in knots. Finally, I stumbled across the section.

Congratulations, Forty-Eight!

We are proud to inform you that your new job at the facility is an Infirmary Technician. You will be stationed on floor 2 working from 2:00 to 9:00 pm, servicing sick patients by setting them up in available clinic rooms.

Your training process will be five days long. Please report to room 404 at 12:00 pm for your daily sessions. Each session will last two hours and go over the basics of the job and our expectations of your performance.

Sincerely,
Margret Heisenberg.

I let out a long breath of relief and slumped down in the chair. Looks like I'd be going back to Headquarters after all. The only issue was finding out how to contact Fifty-Seven, but for now, I was content.

"Cool, I got a uniform designer! Floor two, room 607, from 3:00 to 8:00. What did you all get?" yelled Eighty-Six. Meanwhile, the other two girls didn't look too enthusiastic.

"Storage Helper," replied Eighty-Eight.

"Lunch Organizer," said Seventy-Three.

"I'm an Infirmary Technician," I chimed in all too happily.

"Well, now that we got that out of the way, let's all get set up in our rooms! It's so kind that we're each provided with our own living spaces. Oh, and if anyone needs me, you'll know where to look. I'll be reading a book in bed!" Eighty-Six cheered before giggling off like a schoolgirl.

As everyone dispersed, I decided to find my bedroom so I could take a well-deserved nap. After making two left turns and inching down a narrow hallway, there it was in all its glory. The outside of the door was navy blue and had the label "Forty-Eight" marked across it, confirming that it was indeed mine. Before I could even take in my surroundings, I barged inside and ran straight for the bed. The mattress was just how I remembered, soft and cushiony. My entire body seemed to sink right in when I pounced upon it, and the aches in my back were relieved for just a blissful moment as I drove my face into the pillow. Not even a single thought crossed my mind. As soon as I curled up and felt the warmth of the bed below, I fell into a deep slumber, truly at peace. For once, I wasn't thinking much of anything. No pesky problems that followed me around, no plots or ploys of escape or saving the world. *It was just like home*.

CHAPTER 13

"Rise and shine, girls! Training starts today!"

My head pounded with a rhythmic aching. I quite literally woke up on the wrong side of the bed. Tufts of messy hair jutted in random directions while my body was flailed out in a starfish position. As if that wasn't bad enough, drool lazily fell down the corners of my open mouth while one side of my nose was blocked with morning gunk. Waking up was always the worst part of the day for me, especially with Eighty-Six's obnoxious voice acting as my only alarm clock.

"C'mon, I want to see those determined faces! You may break free from your little caves! And who would want to miss out on a fresh breakfast?"

Breakfast. As grumpy as I was, a good plate of food sounded promising now. I hadn't eaten a proper meal in over two weeks. Hesitantly, I plopped out of bed, untangled myself from under the covers, and staggered over to the door with a limp in my step. However, the aromas from outside instantly cleared my sinuses—bacon and eggs with a big stack of pancakes. A feast fit for a queen! Now that was something I could get used to.

As I stepped into the kitchen, acknowledging my other roommates, a glorious breakfast spread covered every inch of the mahogany table.

"Ta-da! I enjoy a bit of cooking every now and then. Plus, training begins in three hours, so I'd figured it would be nice to have a good start to the day," cheered Eighty-Six.

"Wow, thanks a lot," I muttered, the other two girls agreeing.

"Of course! Bon appétit!"

Immediately, everyone began to dig in. I grabbed all that I could and quickly scarfed everything down, not stopping to catch my breath. It was as if a ravenous beast took control of my body. The only foods I had eaten while stuck in a cell were crackers, whole grain bread with peanut butter, and scrambled eggs on a few special occasions. But *this* spread couldn't even compare.

After the wonderful breakfast, I praised Eighty-Six's skills and hurried to my room to take a hot shower. I felt filthy after staying in the DOD for so long. Letting the warm water flow down my back was the greatest sensation, one of peace and cleanliness. Once I was done, the bathroom was engulfed in clouds of steam, fogging up the mirrors and creating a gentle, misty atmosphere.

I slipped into my new trainee uniform: a blue collared shirt matched with gray sweatpants, and the words "worker in training" etched onto the front pockets. It was strange thinking that I would now be one of them, one of those people who were infamous for their mischievous ways. All this time, I viewed the workers as villains, mad scientists who profited off kids like me. But now, I *was* one, officially part of their team, employed under a boss and a crew of managerial staff. However, this also meant more privileges, a new path of options which seemed to dance right in front of my eyes. There were so many ways that I could abuse the system. I just needed to find the right one.

To pass the time, I decided to make myself comfy and read. In doing so, I took out my favorite book and picked up where I left off. It was called *A Creature's Tail,* the very first story I stumbled upon when I first got here—the large purple book with golden edges and a dragon on the cover. I had been intrigued by the very first sentence, whether it was because of the fantastical elements or the deeper ideas within. "He was but a creature in a cage with no form of escape, crying out to the world below. His deep voice sang with bass and formed nothing but low roars, but his words were seen as that of violent threats to the townspeople." The facility was my cage, and the workers were like townspeople. To them, we were all some vile beasts who deserved nothing but to be poked and prodded day in and day out. No wonder I liked the book so much.

Finally, as 12:00 pm drew near, it was time to begin my training. I put down the novel and stored it behind my pillow, not a rip or tear on its delicate pages. Then, I was up and out the door, making my way to room 404, just like the letter had specified.

The atmosphere outside of the training office was filled with life—vibrant and happy. A large tank filled with aquatic animals flashed bright colors from within the glass as fish and plants swayed to a nonexistent song. Meanwhile, groups of people checked in and out, chatting and discussing work related topics. It was nothing short of comforting.

As I approached the front desk inside, however, my mood immediately shifted. Right there, sitting on the opposite end of the check-in, was none other than Dr. Scarlet Adams. She had on one of her malevolent smiles, waving and smacking gum in her mouth all the while. There appeared to be nobody else in service, meaning that talking to her was my only option. *What a great way to ruin my day.*

"Oh, hello there, Forty-Eight! Glad you're adjusting to your new life as an adult. What can I do for you?" she chirped. The woman acted as if she hadn't tortured me less than two weeks ago.

"I'm here for my 12 o'clock training as an infirmary technician," I replied nonchalantly.

"How lovely. Wait over here until somebody can assist you."

I nodded my head and staggered over to one of the room's metal chairs. As service slowed down, I decided to make some small talk with Scarlet just for the fun of it.

"So, is this where you work all of the time?" I asked.

Her ego looked like it had instantly been shattered. "Actually, no, I'm just filling in for a few sick workers. I could never do a repetitive, mundane job such as this. If you're curious, I am the head manager of data and research for the facility. It is one of the most accomplished titles you can be given. Every day and night, I help to perform experiments and collect some of the most important data that will advance our business," she rambled.

I eventually tuned her out. Boasts and brags went in one ear and out the other. *My* leadership, *my* authority, *my* hard work. A load of garbage I didn't need to hear.

Just when I thought I couldn't take anymore, a worker appeared from the office hallway. "Forty-Eight?" she asked.

"That's me," I replied. *Saved by the bell.*

"Great! I'm all ready for your training. My name is Jordyn Baker, and I will be assisting you for the next five days so you can get prepared for your job at the infirmary. Are you familiar with our structure there?"

"Yes, I visited when I was sick."

"Perfect, so you should know a thing or two about our procedures. I worked as a clinical nurse here for ten years until I moved up to become a trainer, so I'm pretty experienced in this field. You'll be just fine," Jordyn reassured. Her voice was kind and genuine, unlike most of the other workers.

She led me down a white hallway illuminated by bright LED lights until we reached a purple door and turned into her office. The color scheme of the interior was violet and fuchsia, and the walls were covered with inspirational quotes and posters of various cartoons. The rearmost wall, constructed of glass, looked out through the entire chain of offices and training rooms. Besides décor, Jordyn's workspace was the home to a plethora of equipment: tools, flexibility gear, containers of *ElastaGlass,* and prop weapons and drugs.

"Okay, stand right there. Now, let us begin."

The training was simple. I was shown how to work one of the infirmary's computers and check people into available rooms. Jordyn also taught me the mechanics for a few weapons and how to use them. The session lasted about an hour, and once we were done, I made my way down to the cafeteria to grab a quick lunch. A hot sandwich and small cup of apple juice sufficed. Back in my room, I read in the kitchen and waited for the other girls to return from their trainings.

Within thirty minutes, everyone arrived at the complex. Eighty-Six had plenty of stories to share about her wonderful experiences, and I never heard the last of it.

"It was super amazing! I learned how to design uniforms and distribute them around the facility. My instructor was very nice, by the way. Her name is Shelly O'Donnell, and she has pretty jewelry."

All night, she rambled and rambled about the drama and events from her lessons, and even as I crawled into bed, her voice was still ringing in my ears. Thus, the start of a long five-day week had been put into motion.

5 DAYS REMAINING

Finally, the moment I had been waiting for: my first time on the job. After all my training sessions were completed and aced, I was ready to be an infirmary technician for real.

At 2:00 pm, Jordyn greeted me outside of her office and led me down the main stairwell, making the final descent toward Headquarters. The lobby was exactly how I remembered it: labeled sectors, dome glass structures, children chatting at every corner, and of course, my old dormitory, sector D5. No disturbances or discrepancies in sight, nor my old roommate Fifty. Just in the center of it all was the infirmary, the only place that was still in a constant state of rotation. People checked in, people checked out, but not me; I was on the clock.

Once inside, I was shown to my very own desk and workspace. I was also given a designated position behind the counter to assist with customer service.

"There you are, Forty-Eight. Everything's been set up. Good luck!" cheered Jordyn. And with one final affirmation, I was off to begin my duties.

Everything was much faster than I anticipated. As soon as my booth became available, crowds of anxious workers accommodating sick kids swarmed up to my station, hurriedly yelling at me to reserve certain rooms.

"Look lady, I need the biggest room you have ASAP. This boy is about to pass out!"

"Okay, one second, ma'am," I'd reply.

"No, not one second. *Now.* Do you even understand the state he's in?"

"Yes ma'am, but I'm going as fast as the system lets me. It says here that our suite rooms are currently unavailable. Would you be fine with a standard?"

"Of course not! I said the *biggest* room."

"Yes, but unfortunately, I cannot help you there. You can either take the standard or wait until a suite becomes unoccupied."

"How impudent. Can't even help a sick patient."

Many more instances such as this occurred in the span of an hour, and by the time lunch rolled around, I was exhausted.

At 7:30 pm, I finally got the freedom of another short break, so I decided to snoop around my office to get a feel for the new place. It was nothing special, just cubicles and desks, desks and cubicles. However, positioned on one of the walls was a big red phone. In place of numbers, there were buttons to call different sectors, including dorms. And suddenly, a great idea entered my mind, one that was destined to work: all I had to do was dial Fifty-Seven's room. I could tell her everything and formulate a plan with her on the other line. It was a risky scheme, but it was my last and only chance at escape as well as the best opportunity at communication with her.

I surveyed the room to make sure the coast was clear. Hastily, I picked up the receiver and entered the sector name F3 into the phone. It rang for a second, then five, no answer. I reached out a second time. One ring, followed by a continuous three. This time, a minute passed, and there was still no answer. My anxiety shot through the roof, but I didn't give up. I entered in the numbers once more, dialing the dorm. *Third time's the charm.* The awful ringing ceased but instead was replaced with static on the other end. Finally, I heard a girl's voice.

"What do you want? This is the third time you've called," she groaned.

"Is this Fifty-Seven?"

"Not her, sorry. She's my roommate, but I haven't seen her in, like, a month," the voice on the other end replied.

"I'm sorry—*a month*? Where has she been?"

"I don't know, but rumor has it, they're extending her stay."

"Can you please ask around and see where she might be? And call the infirmary once you find her," I begged.

"I mean, sure, but why is she so important to you?"

"I need her for … clinical duties. To run some tests. Also, request you speak with Forty-Eight when you call back."

"Okay, will do."

I hung up the phone, and panic gripped me tightly. Fifty-Seven? Missing? Surely, she should've been brought back to Headquarters by now. A slew of questions whizzed in my mind from left to right. *Where are they keeping her? Did she somehow escape? Why doesn't her roommate know anything?* It was too much to process. From being experimented on in a cell, to being transferred to a dungeon, and then getting employed five days later—it sounded absurd, and it was! Then again, everything about this facility was absurd. The workers were secretive, and I caught on to their schemes from day one. What were they achieving from their studies that was so damn important—immortality? But most of all, why did they need Fifty-Seven and not me? We both participated in the same act of rebellion and stayed in the DOD for ten days, yet here I was, helping others and living in comfortable quarters. Meanwhile, Fifty-Seven was who knows where in some run-down office, playing the role of the helpless lab rat at the hands of these people.

As I continued my shift, all I could do was anxiously wait for the phone to ring. My attention span slowly diminished as the night continued, and I could barely accommodate customers without staring off into space. Luckily, this allowed me to ignore the constant complaints and yelling which seemed to erupt from every visitor that came my way. The sick and the injured, and those who were with them, begged for the biggest rooms, the nicest food, and the best preparations, and I was caught in the crossfire, stuck between my duties and their outright rudeness. The clock ticked in the corner, turning each second into a lulling rhythm, one which teased me and drove me to utter madness. My mind fogged up with polluted thoughts of home, meaningless memories, and plots of escape. Until suddenly, one of my co-workers approached me, red phone in hand.

"Forty-Eight, you got a call."

"Thanks, appreciate it," I replied, taking the device a bit too quickly. In an instant, I stealthily disappeared into the bowels of my office, placing the phone up to my ear while I fiddled with locks of hair.

"Hello, you've reached Forty-Eight, infirmary technician. How may I help you?" I asked in my stateliest manner.

"Hey, it's Fifty-Seven's roommate again. Some of the guards told me that they took her into sector X2 for testing or something. But that's all they said."

"Okay, X2… testing, got it. Thanks a lot," I blurted, breaking my professional persona.

Before letting the girl get another chance to speak, I hung up the phone, practically skipping my way back to the check-in. Thankfully, it was 8:49 pm, just eleven minutes before work ended. Service had become drastically slower compared to the afternoon, and soon, it seemed like almost nobody was even coming to the infirmary. That left just me and my thoughts. To be honest, I had not the slightest clue how I was going to break Fifty-Seven out of sector X2 and make it back in one piece. I already knew that the run-and-go method always ended up in disaster. However, I wasn't limited in options. This time, *I'd just have to hide in plain sight*. With my rise in the social hierarchy, making my way around would be much easier. I now had access to uniforms, permission to use certain devices, and information about short-cut routes throughout the lobby—things like that. I could pretend to be a higher-up or even the daughter of a well-respected worker so they'd instantly respect *me*. It would be the perfect disguise. No more hiding or sneaking around in hard-to-see areas. Instead, everyone would simply look right through me without a care in the world.

That night, I ended my shift at 9:00 pm and went back to my room. It was past curfew for the people at Headquarters, a whopping hour before our curfew even began. As I approached my room on the floor of the Landing, I could barely contain my excitement and anxiousness, and although unable to sleep, I tried to pass out on my bed. All that resulted was a night full of tossing and turning, wondering what was to come next.

Such was the life of Stella Winterfield, AKA Forty-Eight.

CHAPTER 14

4 DAYS REMAINING

As I woke up from my restless slumber, Eighty-Six's voice reverberated throughout the complex in a sing-song manner. Stories and gossip, events which unfolded yesterday, she raved about it all. Knowing full well I wouldn't fall back asleep, I decided to enter the kitchen and make some small talk with my roommates. As I drew closer, Eighty-Six was excitedly gushing over her new position as a uniform designer once again.

"Yes, my job is great! I produced so many different outfits. Turns out, they have special attire for the higher ups, made of deluxe silk… oh, good morning Forty-Eight! How was your first day?" she asked upon seeing me.

"It was good. Crazy but good," I replied. Eighty-Six smiled and resumed her conversation with Eighty-Eight.

Listening to her mindless babble proved beneficial to me when a lightbulb went off in my head. The new escape plan I made on the spot last night didn't seem so farfetched anymore. If I were to hide in plain sight, I'd surely need a disguise, and it just so happened that my roommate worked in that area of expertise: a uniform designer. She was exactly the person I needed for a mission like this.

"Hey, Eighty-Six? Were you saying something about deluxe uniforms just now?" I questioned.

"Yes, why?"

"Well, I … need an outfit for one of the people at the infirmary. She's the manager of research, and she actually performs experiments and collects some important data for the facility." I was shocked by my own words. Scarlet Adams's previous boasts from the day before were pouring out of my mouth like info vomit. *Anything to stick to my plan.*

"Oh, of course! But for someone like that, I'll have to use the premium silks, and my boss told me yesterday that we were due for a restock. It might take a few to finish, if that's okay."

"That's completely fine. Take all the time you need." I chuckled, knowing damn well that I only had four days left to live. It seemed like just last night I was arriving on the conveyer belts, lost and confused. *Oh, what a journey it's been.*

I've been involved in so many scandals, so many plots, so many pitiful plans at escaping. If only I had known from the beginning that the exits were a hoax. Maybe I wouldn't have risked my well-being and put everything on the line for a half-baked plan. Then again, I wondered what my life would've been like if I never fell into a coma in the first place. I'd probably be living happily, hitting up all the beaches and local attractions. Mia would be with me, laughing and joking all the way. And on my eighteenth birthday: a day of chaos with no limits. I'd be with my friends, sneaking drinks, dancing, doing it all, but instead, my mother was probably crying over my death. Of course, I wasn't actually dead. Not yet.

13 HOURS REMAINING

Today was the day, my last chance at escaping. Luckily, the night before, Eighty-Six came back with my prized possession: a fancy silk uniform paired with a baby blue skirt. I'd spent all morning getting into character, as I was no longer Forty-Eight, nor Stella Winterfield. Instead, I would be playing the role of Evalie Heisenberg, Margret's fake daughter. I had heard that Margret did, in fact, have a daughter, but no one knew anything about her. My entire story was mapped out from start to finish, and I practiced in the mirror too many times to count.

"Hello there, I'm Evalie Heisenberg. I was sent here to look at Fifty-Seven and possibly transfer her to another room. See, there are more subjects on the waiting list, and my manager told me we needed to accommodate this space for others. Oh, take this. I have a note signed by my mother." It was the perfect farce.

8 HOURS REMAINING

It was 3:00 pm, and here I was working my final day on the job as an Infirmary Technician.

As soon as my shift ends, I plan on wasting no time at all in order to get into disguise.

2 HOURS REMAINING

9:00 pm arrived, my shift ended, and thus, I was able to go back to my complex. I practically ran the entire way there. As soon as I stepped foot through the door, I locked myself in the bedroom and rushed to put on my outfit.

The silk shirt slipped on haphazardly as it was two sizes too big, yet I just had to go with it. Likewise, when it came to the skirt, I experienced the same problems, as it was dangerously loose when it rested atop my hips. However, this time, I used part of a wire hanger as a makeshift pin to clip it tight around my waist, securing the bottom half of the outfit as to where it fit like a snug pillow. Finally, to finish off the fake look, I tied my hair into an obnoxious ponytail, mirroring Margret's awful blonde mop. *Like mother, like daughter, they say.* And oh, how I played the part! Everything about my costume screamed Evalie, from the baby blue attire, to the pompous updo. It was a disguise like no other, or a genius coverup if I were to say so myself. Although it was only a quarter 'til 10:00 pm, I felt ready to escape. I, Stella Winterfield, was prepared and dedicated to go all out as Margret's nonexistent daughter. Repeatedly, I repeated the plan to myself: go downstairs to Headquarters right before 10:00 pm to avoid the staircase barriers. Then, make my surprise entrance not too shortly after. When I arrive, do my song and dance about how I'm Evalie, take Fifty-Seven, and run for the coma machines in Z9. It had some rough patches, but it was all that I had left.

1 HOUR AND 5 MINUTES REMAINING

At last, the time arrived, five minutes before 10:00 pm. Without skipping a beat, I hurried out of my room and bid it farewell, the walls painted light blue, the mahogany doorframe, for it would be the last I'd ever see it again. My roommates hadn't arrived from their shifts either, meaning that they, too, would be removed from my memory, a figment of my days spent at the facility. It sure was a shame.

As I ran through the futuristic hallways of the Landing, the ones that contained gadgets and high-tech interfaces, I felt out of place. There was something in the atmosphere that activated my fight or flight response, and I was never sure if it was the cameras that watched me with their metal eyes, or the workers who seemed like robots themselves, almost scanning for bugs in my DNA. Nonetheless, I always knew that it wasn't home. Sure, I'd adapted to *calling* it my home, but when your own memory is wiped clean from your brain and you don't know anything else besides your current reality, it's quite hard not to. Although ever since the very beginning, my body always fought back. Even when I didn't know my name, my family, or even my own personality, short recaps, almost like visions, would fog up my mind and reveal small details about my life. But once I remembered Mia and my mother, they stopped happening all together. I guess that goes to show that they *were* my entire life; family over everything else. Little did they know *I was coming back home*.

I ran across the lobby and finally reached the staircase and the same damn corridor with ominous shadows and creatures that lurked below. As I made my descent, I was cautious to not make much noise, gliding my feet across the ground in a secretive manner all the way down to Headquarters.

To my luck, the first floor was a barren wasteland, a ghost town of sorts. Not a person was stirring After Hours, like I had the entire lobby to myself. All I needed to do was make my way toward sector X2, although that was easier said than done. A note with Margret's forged signature was clasped into my right hand, and I trembled with fear and anxiety. Sweat beads dripped down my face. *I never recall HQ being this hot before.* Not only that, but there was something different in the way I stepped. No longer did I roll in on confident strides but jerky movements as my bones shook and my hands mindlessly fidgeted. Every time my feet hit the floor, a knot formed within my chest, like it could explode at any moment.

Left foot.

Right foot.

Only forward as I pushed through the lobby, not as Stella Winterfield, but Evalie Heisenberg. I passed by all the different sectors, and suddenly found myself approaching the line of U's. The U's turned into V's, and the V's turned into W's, and before I knew it, I was standing directly outside of sector X2.

30 MINUTES REMAINING

The door was a dark gray metal and gave off an intimidating presence. Just being in its vicinity induced anxiety chills. A looming aura, one of doom and dread, gave the atmosphere a very unsettling quality, to the point where I knew that I wasn't supposed to be there. It felt as if, at any moment, someone would lurch from the shadows and snatch me up in one fell swoop to escort me to my impending doom. My stomach flipped upside down. My breath hitched in my throat. It was now or never.

Knock. Knock. Knock.

The metal was cold against my knuckles. For a second, I wanted to just run away, forget about escaping, and die a peaceful death. But before I could make that choice, somebody answered the door.

"Excuse me, can I help you? Nobody is supposed to be out this late at night," the woman said. She had jet black hair wrapped into a neat bun and almond shaped eyes which accentuated her icy glare. Meanwhile, a nametag on the front of her blouse read, "Antoinette Bordeaux: Manager of Immortality Studies."

"Um… yes. I am Evalie Heisenberg, daughter of Dr. Heisenberg. I was sent out to perform a routine inspection on one of your subjects," I stammered.

"Well, unfortunately, Marget doesn't talk about her daughter very often. Do you have any form of verification?"

"Yes, ma'am. I have this note right here," I blurted, quickly handing over the faux sheet of paper. It was a facility edition loose leaf slip with gold edgings and a forged signature, one that I practiced repeatedly from my job offer letter.

"Very well, let's take a look," she said as she licked her lips, reading off the sheet. "This pass is issued to Evalie Heisenberg under the MLD department of safety to issue a routine check-up on patients in testing. Signed, MHB… alright."

I furiously fidgeted with my hands as the woman looked me up and down.

"Okay then, you may come inside but don't take too long. And please don't mess with any of the equipment."

Success.

As I entered the room, the sudden drop in temperature chilled me to my core. The lab was small and filled with various types of equipment and technology, things that I wouldn't have been able to imagine in my wildest fantasies before I arrived at this place. Trinkets and gizmos, extreme light fixtures and robots; they had it all. Standing watch in the corner were groups of elders jotting down notes on clipboards, and occasionally nodding or exclaiming subtle oohs and ahhs. Besides that, everything seemed normal. I diverted my attention to the center of the room. Between all the scientists and cluttered equipment stood a grand machine. It resembled a box of sorts that was closed off on three sides by solid walls. The side which wasn't closed faced away from me, so that all I could see was a flat structure, whereas the group of researchers were all huddled in front, marveling at something on the other end. It was odd.

"Excuse me, everybody, stop what you're doing," the woman shouted. "Dr. Heisenberg's daughter has come to perform a routine inspection. I need you to shut this all down."

"Yes, ma'am," their voices echoed.

The scientists dispersed from their arrangement and scattered around the lab, unplugging various cords and flipping switches. Very abruptly, the machine in the center stopped buzzing, and the room fell into a quiet and collective hush. One of the male workers gestured for me to approach the contraption, moving out of the aisle.

As I turned the corner around the mysterious box, my suspicions grew. Solid, beige confinements hid away something of utmost importance. Meanwhile, moving closer, I got a strange gut feeling. The lights flickered. Loose wires seemed to writhe like snakes. The walls were closing in as I held my breath and counted to three.

One… *it can't be that bad.*

Two… *you know what to expect.*

Three…

The other end of the machine looked like something straight out of my nightmares. A girl had been placed on top of a blue tube, completely motionless. Her skin was sickly pale, and she looked so delicate, as if a papercut would make her bleed out. However, upon closer inspection, I realized that she wasn't just *any* girl.

She was Fifty-Seven.

But not the Fifty-Seven I remembered, that's for sure.

"I'm sorry. What's going on here?" I asked, trying to keep my composure.

"Well, you see, we've been trying to extend this young girl's stay at the facility, and this device helps keep her body intact," said one of the male scientists.

"Okay, and are you aware how old this machine is?"

"Um, no, I suppose we don't know," said another.

"Seriously? It looks rusted. That's breaking the worker code of conduct for not ensuring patient safety." My voice boomed with authority. It felt strange being in such a high position of power, even if I was just pretending to be someone I wasn't.

"Well, what do you suggest we do?"

"There's nothing that can be done unless I speak with the subject personally and in private. It's to make sure that you haven't been neglecting her needs."

Suddenly, one of the elders backed up, a nasty look on her face. "Unfortunately, a private conversation is not possible. Unless you have an authorized form of verification, we are not permitted to leave this room unattended."

"If I remember correctly, I do have an authorized form of verification. It was my pass, wasn't it?" I teased.

"No, a silly slip of paper will not give you the same privileges that I've worked my entire life for," she argued.

"Ladies, quiet down," shouted Antoinette above all the commotion. "With all due respect, Miss Heisenberg is in possession of a facility-issued permit. Therefore, she has every right to privately communicate with our patient here. That being said, Helen, would you please step aside?"

Helen huffed and mumbled a few swears under her breath before getting out of my way.

"Thank you. Now, Mark, please release Fifty-Seven from the chamber," instructed Dr. Bordeaux.

This time, a middle-aged man wearing a lab coat arose from the crowd. He approached the back of the machine and opened a hidden door that connected to the chamber—the same tube which held Fifty-Seven. Upon stepping outside, she made a few wobbly movements, like she hadn't walked in days, and was assisted down the aisle with the help of the scientist.

"Alright everybody, you know the drill. Let's give these two some time to talk," announced Antoinette. All the workers muttered in agreement before clambering outside the room, shutting the door behind them. That just left me and Fifty-Seven.

The first few seconds were completely silent, like we had this sense of *knowing*. Her eyes expressed all her inner thoughts, although cloudy and glazed over with a slight film. Any other person would've said she looked emotionless, but to me, I understood everything. It was ironic, as we hadn't known each other for too long, yet somehow we bonded over one mutual connection: the desire and passionate will to live. However, something inside me felt off when I was around her. Since the day we met, she always seemed so vaguely familiar, from the way she talked, the way she walked, and the way she spoke. It was like we were destined to meet.

I decided to break the tension and speak first, asking a question I had for a while now. "So, what the hell happened?"

Fifty-Seven looked more timid. She shuffled her feet aimlessly while breaking eye contact, like she was scared of something. "I don't know. I was sent to the Direct Order Dormitory, and they told me I'd be released after ten days. Except, something happened. It was weird because suddenly, they were so interested in my DNA, my physical traits, and whatever. And so, they brought me here to do even more tests. At first, they said it would only be for two days. Two days go by, and all is good. But then they tell me they're extending my stay, this time for an undetermined period. I get put into this damn machine, where all I do is sit and watch. Meanwhile, the rest of *them* observe me like I'm a zoo animal, just on display for all to see. Not once did they ever explain why. It was a lot of hushed conversation and frantic glares. Man, I don't even know why you came back for me. I die in a few minutes, anyway. It's pointless."

"No, you're wrong," I whisper yelled. "Because I know a way out. There is no physical escape because we are in a coma—a simulation! Look, I know this sounds crazy, but I found an official diary from the owner himself. It held all the answers to our questions, every last one. And as it turns out, there is no physical escape from here. Instead, they have exit devices in sector Z9. It's the only way we can wake up. Oh, and this disguise, all this Evalie Heisenberg bullshit, is just some elaborate ruse to get us there. Just think, Antionette fell for it. If the manager can believe it, anyone can!" I exclaimed. Fifty-Seven cracked a small smile. "What do you say? Are you ready to get the hell out of here?"

"Yeah, of course," she replied.

"Atta-girl! That's the spirit. Let me get those snobby scientists back in here so we can get things moving. All you have to do is follow my lead."

She nodded as I approached the front entrance to the lab, the door open ever so slightly. The workers on the other side had suspicious looks on their faces, as if they were watching out for something, waiting.

"Hey guys, you're free to come back inside." I gestured. They simply grunted and groaned as they all tried to squeeze through the doorway.

Once everyone was back in their assembled groups, I stood in the center of the lab and loudly cleared my throat.

"Okay, I have bad news. About half of the machinery in this room is against MLD protocol, and it doesn't help that our patient here was unsatisfied with her treatment. That being said, I can do one of two things. The first option is to bring up this issue to Dr. Marwood," I said as a collective gasp echoed throughout the room, "or I can transfer Fifty-Seven to a different lab and pretend that this never happened. You all can make your decisions now, and it *is* majority rule."

The team whispered for about five seconds, then turned to face me while collectively shouting their responses. The words "choice two" repeated in my ears like a sweet song, and for a moment, I felt like an almighty figure; I was taking authority over those who had wronged me.

"Okay, the decision has been made! Well, thank you all for your cooperation. I'll be taking Fifty-Seven, now," I blurted, grabbing her by the shoulder and moving along.

7 MINUTES REMAINING

I frantically pushed past the door, speed walking my way out of sector X2 and into the vastness of the lobby. However, just when I thought I'd finally gotten away with it, Antoinette, along with some other scientists, decided to tag along.

"Excuse me," Dr. Bordeaux yelled. "Not so fast. I have a few questions I'd like to ask you."

Of course.

I stopped in my tracks and approached Antoinette, a bit of malevolence present in my fake smile.

"Yes? What is it?" I innocently asked.

"Well, first of all, I'd like to know where you're going," she answered coldly.

"Oh... just sector Z1."

"Z1, huh? Funny, considering that's a storage room."

"Oh, sorry, did I say Z1? I meant Y1."

Save.

"Hmm, very well. Next up, do you know of a young girl named Eighty-Six?"

I visibly gulped as my face turned pale with horror. *There's no way they could possibly know. I played all my cards so carefully.* Still, a bunch of questions and doubt overflowed in my mind.

"I take your silence as a no. Here, let me restate that… do you know anyone who is roommates with Eighty-Six?"

This wasn't happening.

"Um, Eighty-Eight, Seventy-Three, and…" I started, my voice slowly fading.

"And? There's one more."

Sweat dripped down my face. My breathing faltered as I stared off into Antoinette's piercing gray eyes.

5 MINUTES REMAINING

"Fine, I might as well enlighten you. It's another young girl named Forty-Eight. Have you heard of her?"

"Yes, I … believe so."

"Great! Well, tell me this Evalie. Do you know what happened to Forty-Eight?" Dr. Bordeaux paused and tapped her chin in faux confusion. "That's right. She tried to escape. And do you know what happened when she got caught?"

I was completely motionless. My eyes didn't blink. My lungs didn't take in a breath. My heart didn't beat. I couldn't speak.

"Well, *I guess we're about to find out.*"

Everything happened in slow motion. I watched as Antoinette reached for a gun in her waist strap. I grabbed Fifty-Seven and ran.

Left foot.
Right foot.
My feet hit the floor in rhythmic beats. A few pops went off in the distance. I just kept moving. The constant thought of sector Z9 replayed in my mind. We needed to get there. We needed to escape.

Z9 came into view from far away. Meanwhile, groups of workers once again chased us through the lobby as we ran. I simply ignored them. Fifty-Seven still held a tight grip on my arm, and I made sure not to make the same mistake this time around like our prior escape attempts.

3 MINUTES REMAINING

Finally, we reached the door of the sector. I pushed it open with extreme force and dragged Fifty-Seven inside with me. However, the room wasn't what we expected. One single Comatiz chair stood idle in the center along with its tools and remotes. That meant one thing—only one of us could go home.

The commotion outside got louder as the workers drew near.

"Forty-Eight, get in the damn chair! What are you waiting for?" yelled Fifty-Seven.

"What about you?" I shouted back.

"Don't worry about me. I'll take care of the others," she yelled.

2 MINUTES REMAINING

I hopped onto the chair and pressed the "on" button. It instantly hummed and buzzed and came to life with crackling sounds. Meanwhile, Fifty-Seven boarded up the door with loose boxes, machines, and whatever else she could get her hands on.

"Take the two wires with suctions, stick them to your forehead, and click the red button on the remote next to you." I recited all that I had remembered from the entries in the book. Meanwhile, the stampede outside was no longer in the distance. They would be on top of us at any second.

Quickly, I placed the suctions on my forehead while grabbing the side remote. There was no more thinking involved. Sweat poured down my face, and my heart felt like it would explode from my chest. Finally, I pushed the red button and closed my eyes. This was it. I was finally going to be free from this hell. The anticipation rose from within me as images of home crossed my mind. I became impatient. The machine buzzed. The electricity whirred. The world spun in circles around the room and consumed me into its dark abyss.

Goodbye, Facility.

Goodbye, Fifty-Seven…

Slowly, I opened my eyes, only to be met with disappointment. I was still in the chair in sector Z9. Fifty-Seven was still boarding up the door. The group was still chasing after us. *The machine didn't work.*

1 MINUTE REMAINING

"Hey, it's not working! What the hell do I do?" I screamed.

"Just keep doing what you're doing!"

"But there's not enough time. You won't be able to escape!"

But I suspect we knew that all along.

"Dammit, listen to me!" shouted Fifty-Seven. Her back pressed against the door with all her might. "I don't even know how to use that machine. It's useless! You need to get out of here! I'm sorry that I was wrong about escaping this place.

And I'm sorry that I can't go with you. Just stay alive for me. That's all I'm asking!" Tears streamed down her face.

20 SECONDS REMAINING

"I'll come back for you," I said above the noise in the room, and I pushed the button again.

Subtle vibrations shocked me from side to side, and suddenly, the light of the machine burned brighter, like a spark igniting.

"There it is! Keep using the remote!" she yelled.

15 SECONDS REMAINING

The crowd of workers were upon us. They smashed the wooden door repeatedly until it chipped off into several large pieces. Fifty-Seven kept her back pressed to it as her screams reverberated throughout the room.

There was still one more question I had amid the chaos and confusion. It was something I wanted to ask for a long time.

5 SECONDS REMAINING

"Fifty-Seven, who are you?"

"Elliana… my name's Elliana!"

I pushed the big red button one last time. A spark jolted throughout my entire body as flashes and sensations bombarded my brain. I flashed a smile of pure happiness.

"I'm Stella, Stella Winterfield!"

And then, everything went black.

The loud noises of a busy hospital echoed throughout the building. Bright fluorescent lights gave the room a strong glow while beeping machines broke through the cacophony of sound coming from every direction.

A nurse wearing blue scrubs walked into the room, an excited look on her face. "She's finally awake!"

It had been the happiest day of Clara Winterfield's life. Her beautiful daughter was healthy and strong, and she couldn't have asked for anything more perfect.

Stella Winterfield.

"Oh, it looks like she's hungry," said the nurse as the baby she rocked in her arms began to softly cry. "You know, Stella is a very cute name for a newborn."

"I know! She's everything I hoped for," exclaimed her mother.

It had only been one week since the birth of her daughter on July 30, 2005, and the events of that night still played fresh in Clara's mind.

As for Stella, that meant yet another failed attempt.

She was now on trial twenty. After her death on August 9, 2022, the cycle began again for her once more. She had experienced life and death again and again and again, yet she just couldn't seem to escape from the facility.

But at least for now, and for the next seventeen years, she would be home.

BOOK CLUB QUESTIONS

1. Stella wakes up with no memory of who she is. How does the novel explore the connection between memory and identity? Do you think we are still ourselves if we forget everything about our past?

2. From the moment Stella wakes up, the facility is shrouded in secrecy. What were your initial theories about where she was and why? How did your guesses evolve as the story progressed?

3. Stella is trapped in an unknown place, and she must navigate her surroundings to survive. How does her experience compare to traditional survival stories? What makes this different?

4. The title suggests a ticking clock. How does the passage of time affect Stella's mental and emotional state? Did you feel the pacing of the novel built tension effectively?

5. The story begins with Stella and her sister running from a bombing. How did that opening set the tone for the rest of the novel? In what ways does the attack shape Stella's actions and emotions later?

6. As Stella tries to piece together what happened, she encounters obstacles and potential threats. How does the novel explore themes of paranoia and trust? Were there any moments where you questioned who (or what) she could rely on?

7. The book is described as a dark sci-fi tale reminiscent of *Severance* and *Lost*. Do you see the influence of these shows in the story? What similar themes or storytelling techniques stand out?

8. The phrase "Left foot... Right foot..." appears often throughout the story. What do you think this mantra represents for Stella? How does it reflect her mindset and journey?

9. Fear is a major element in the novel, both in terms of the unknown and the facility itself. How does fear shape Stella's decisions? Did her reactions to the facility's mysteries feel realistic to you?

10. Without giving away spoilers, did the ending satisfy you? Were all your questions answered, or were there lingering mysteries? If there's a sequel, what do you think will happen next?

AUTHOR BIO

Morgan DeVivo is a teenage debut author from Tampa, Florida. She has always had a passion for science fiction and writing, starting her journey as an author in middle school. Her first book, *40 Days*, is a thrilling young adult science fiction novel that is sure to captivate readers. When not writing, Morgan likes to draw and edit videos. With a strong passion for storytelling and a unique perspective, Morgan is an exciting new voice in the world of young adult literature.

Discover more at
4HorsemenPublications.com

10% off using HORSEMEN10